"You're [ ] Shotgun Wedding...?" She Asked, Her Brow Raised.

"Something like that," he admitted.

Stephanie shook her head. "Thanks for stopping by, Alec. You're an honorable man. But your baby is safe in my hands. I'll drop you a line once it's born."

"Not quite the way things are going to happen," he said as he stared down at her with intense purpose. "Get this straight in your mind, Stephanie. You *are* marrying me."

She squinted into his dark, intense eyes. "That was a joke, right?"

"Am I laughing?"

Dear Reader,

Welcome to book number three in the MONTANA
MILLIONAIRES: THE RYDERS series from Silhouette
Desire. I have a great time writing siblings, and I hope you
enjoy Stephanie's story in *His Convenient Virgin Bride,*
along with the stories of her brothers, Royce and Jared,
in the companion books.

I also love a ranch setting and a smart, protective hero.
Add to that a little mystery and a long-ago family secret,
and you have the ingredients for a really fun write. I
enjoyed exploring the Ryder family history in this book, and
it was great to touch base again with the characters from
Seduction and the CEO and *In Bed with the Wrangler.*

I hope you enjoy the finale to the Ryders' series.

Happy reading!

Barbara

BARBARA DUNLOP

HIS CONVENIENT VIRGIN BRIDE

Published by Silhouette Books
America's Publisher of Contemporary Romance

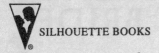 SILHOUETTE BOOKS

Recycling programs
for this product may
not exist in your area.

ISBN-13: 978-0-373-73022-3

HIS CONVENIENT VIRGIN BRIDE

Visit Silhouette Books at www.eHarlequin.com

Printed in U.S.A.

Books by Barbara Dunlop

Silhouette Desire

Thunderbolt over Texas #1704
Marriage Terms #1741
The Billionaire's Bidding #1793
The Billionaire Who Bought Christmas #1836
Beauty and the Billionaire #1853
Marriage, Manhattan Style #1897
Transformed Into the Frenchman's Mistress #1929
*Seduction and the CEO #1996
*In Bed with the Wrangler #2003
*His Convenient Virgin Bride #2009

*Montana Millionaires: The Ryders

BARBARA DUNLOP

writes romantic stories while curled up in a log cabin in Canada's far north, where bears outnumber people and it snows six months of the year. Fortunately, she has a brawny husband and two teenage children to haul firewood and clear the driveway while she sips cocoa and muses about her upcoming chapters. Barbara loves to hear from readers. You can contact her through her Web site at www.barbaradunlop.com.

For my husband

One

Stephanie Ryder felt a telltale breeze puff against the skin of her chest. She glanced down to discover a button had popped on her stretch cotton blouse. The lace of her white bra and the curve of her breasts were clearly visible in the gap.

She crossed her arms to block the view, arching a mocking brow at the man silhouetted in the tack shed door. "You, Alec Creighton, are no gentleman."

Wearing a dress shirt, charcoal slacks and black loafers that were at odds with the rustic setting of a working horse stable, his gaze moved indolently from the wall of her forearm back to her eyes. "It took you twenty-four hours to figure that out?"

"Hardly," she scoffed. "But you keep reinforcing the impression."

He took a step forward. "Are you still mad?"

She swiftly redid the button and smoothed her blouse. "I was never mad."

Disappointed, yes. Wesley Harrison had been inches away from kissing her last night when Alec had interrupted them.

Wesley was a great guy. He was good-looking, smart and funny, and only a year younger than Stephanie. He'd been training at Ryder Equestrian Center since June, and he'd been flirting with her since they met.

"He's too young for you," said Alec.

"We're the same age." Practically.

The jut of Alec's brow questioned her honesty, but he didn't call her on it.

With his trim hair, square chin, slate-gray eyes and instructions to go through her equestrian business records with a fine-tooth comb, she should have found his presence intimidating. But Stephanie had spent most of her life handling two older brothers and countless unruly jumping horses. She wasn't about to get rattled by a hired corporate gun.

"Shouldn't you be working?" she asked.

"I need your help."

It was her turn to quirk a brow. Financial management was definitely not her forte. "With what?"

"Tour of the place."

She reached for the cordless phone on the workbench next to Rosie-Jo's tack. "No problem." She pressed speed dial three.

"What are you doing?"

The numbers bleeped swiftly in her ear. "Calling the stable manager."

Alec closed the distance between them. "Why?"

"To arrange for a tour."

He lifted the phone from her hand and pressed the off button. "You can give me a tour."

"I don't have time."

"You are still mad at me."

"No, I'm not."

She wasn't thrilled to have him here. Who would be? He'd be her houseguest for the next few days, and he was under orders from her brothers to streamline the family's corporation, Ryder International. She was a little worried, okay a *lot* worried, that he'd find fault with her management of the Ryder Equestrian Center.

Stephanie didn't skimp on quality, which meant she didn't skimp on cost, either. She was training world-class jumpers. And competing at that level demanded the best in everything; horses, feed, tack, trainers, vets and facilities. She was accustomed to defending her choices to her brothers. She wasn't crazy about defending them to a stranger.

"Are you proud of the place?" he asked.

"Absolutely," she answered without hesitation.

"Then show it to me," he challenged.

She hesitated, searching her mind for a dignified out.

He waited, the barest hint of a smirk twitching his mouth.

Finally she squared her shoulders, straightened to her full five foot five and met his gaze head-on. "You, Alec Creighton," she repeated, "are no gentleman."

The smile broadened, and he eased away, stepping to one side and gesturing to the tack shed door. "After you."

Stephanie waltzed past with her head held high.

It wasn't often a man talked her into a corner. She didn't much like it, but she might as well get this over with. She'd give him his tour, answer his questions, send him back to the ranch house office and get back to her regular routine.

She had an intermediate jumping class to teach this morning, her own training this afternoon and she needed to have the vet examine her Hanoverian mare, Rosie-Jo. Rosie had shied at a jump in practice yesterday, and Stephanie needed to make sure the horse didn't have any hidden injuries.

They headed down the dirt road alongside a hay barn, moving in the direction of the main stable and riding arena. She was tempted to lead him, expensive loafers and all, through the mud and manure around the treadmill pool.

It would serve him right.

"So, what exactly is it that you do?" she asked, resisting temptation.

"I troubleshoot."

She tipped her head to squint at his profile in the bright sunshine. Last night, she'd privately acknowledged that he was an incredibly good-looking man. He also carried himself well, squared shoulders, long stride, confident gait. "And what does that mean?"

"It means, that when people have trouble, they call me." He nodded to the low, white building, off by itself at the edge of Melody Meadow. "What's that?"

"Vet clinic. What kind of trouble?"

"Your kind of trouble. You have your own vet?"

"We do. You mean cash flow and too rapid corporate expansion?" That was the Ryder's corporate issue in a nutshell.

"Sometimes."

"And the other times?"

He didn't answer.

"Are you proud of it?" she goaded.

He gave a rueful smile as he shook his head.

She tilted her head to one side, going for ingenuous and hopeful. It usually worked on her brothers.

"Fine. Mostly I identify market sector expansion opportunities then analyze the financial and political framework of specific overseas economic regions."

She blinked.

"On behalf of privately held companies."

"The vet's name is Dr. Anderson," she offered.

Alec coughed out a chuckle.

"It sounds challenging," she admitted, turning her focus back to the road.

He shrugged. "You need to develop contacts. But once you learn the legislative framework of a given county, it applies to all sorts of situations."

"I suppose it would."

The breeze freshened, while horses whinnied as they passed a row of paddocks.

"Tell me about your job," Alec prompted.

"I teach horses to jump over things," she stated, not even attempting to dress it up.

There was a smile in his voice, but his tone was mild. "That sounds challenging."

"Not at all. You get them galloping really fast, point them at a jump and most of the time they figure it out."

"And if they don't?"

"Then they stop, and you keep going."

"Headfirst?" he asked.

"Headfirst."

"Ouch."

She subconsciously rubbed the tender spot on the outside of her right thigh where she'd landed hard coming off Rosie-Jo yesterday. "Ouch is right."

The road tapered to a trail as they came up to the six-foot, white rail fence that surrounded the main riding arena. Alec paused to watch a group of young jumping students and their trainer on the far side.

Stephanie stopped beside him.

"I didn't mean to sound pretentious," he offered.

"I know." She had no doubt that he was accurately describing his job. Her brothers wouldn't have hired him if he wasn't a skilled and experienced professional.

Alec hooked his hand over the top fence rail and pivoted to face her. "So, are you going to tell me what you really do?"

Stephanie debated another sarcastic answer, but there was a frankness in his slate eyes that stopped her.

"I train horses," she told him. "I buy horses, sell horses, board them, breed them and train them." She shifted her gaze to the activities of the junior class. "And I jump them."

"I hear you're headed for the Olympics." His gaze was intent on her expression.

"The Olympics are a long way off. I'm focused on the Brighton competition for the moment."

As she spoke, Wesley appeared from behind the bleachers, leading Rockfire into the arena for a round of jumps. Even from this distance, she could appreciate his fresh-faced profile, lanky body and sunshine-blond hair.

His lips had been *that* close to hers.

She wondered if he'd try again.

"What about management?"

Stephanie blinked her focus back to Alec. "Hmm?"

"Management. I assume you also manage the stable operations?"

She nodded, her gaze creeping sideways for another

glimpse of Wesley as he mounted his horse. This was his first year on the adult jumping circuit, and he was poised to make a splash. He grinned as he spoke to Tina, the junior class instructor, raking a spread hand through his full, tousled hair before putting on his helmet.

"Your boyfriend?" There was an edge to Alec's voice.

Stephanie turned guiltily, embarrassed that her attention had wandered.

Alec frowned at her, and the contrast between the two men was startling. One light, one dark. One carefree, one intense.

She shook her head. "No."

"Just a crush then?"

"It's nothing."

Alec dropped his hand from the rail as Wesley and Rockfire sailed over the first jump. "It's something."

She glared at him. "It's none of your business, is what it is."

He stared back for a silent minute.

His eyes were dark. His lips were parted. And a fissure of awareness suddenly sizzled through her.

No.

Not Alec.

It was Wesley she wanted.

"You're right," Alec conceded into the long silence. "It is none of my business."

None of his business, Alec reminded himself.

Back inside her house that evening, he found himself staring at Stephanie's likeness in a framed cover of *Equine Earth* magazine that was hanging on the living room wall. The fact that her silver-blue eyes seemed to hide enchanting secrets, that her unruly, auburn hair begged for a man's touch and that the light spray of freckles across her nose lent a sense of vulnerability to an otherwise flawless face, was none of his damn business.

The equestrian trophy in her hand, however, was his business, as was the fact that the Ryder name was sprayed across the cover of a nationally circulated magazine.

"That was at Carlton Shores," came her voice, its resonance sending a buzz of awareness up his spine.

"Two thousand and eight," she finished, coming up beside him.

He immediately caught the scent of fresh brewed coffee, and looked over to see two burgundy, stoneware mugs in her hands.

"You won," he stated unnecessarily.

She handed him one of the mugs. "You seem like a 'black' kind of a guy."

He couldn't help but smile at her accurate assessment. "Straight to the heart of the matter," he agreed.

"I take cream and sugar." She paused. "Dress it up as much as you can, I guess."

"Why does that not surprise me?"

She was in a business that was all pomp, glitz and show. Oh, she worked hard at it. There was no way she would have made it this far if she hadn't. But her division of Ryder International certainly wasn't the bedrock of the company's income stream.

He took a sip of the coffee. It was just the way he liked it, robust, without being sharp on the tongue.

She followed suit, and his gaze took a tour from her damp, freshly washed hair, pulled back in a sensible braid, to her clingy, white tank top and the pair of comfortable navy sweatpants that tapered down to incongruous lime-green socks.

"Nice," he observed.

She grinned, sticking a foot forward to show it off. "Royce brought them back for me from London. Apparently they're all the rage."

"You're making a fashion statement?"

"Everything else was in the laundry," she admitted. "I'm kind of lazy that way."

"Right. Lazy. That was the first thing I thought when I met you." It was nearly nine o'clock in the evening, and she'd only just stopped work to come in and shower for dinner.

"I'm going to assume that was sarcasm."

"The outfit works," he told her sincerely. Quite frankly, with her compact curves and toned muscles, she'd make a sackcloth work just fine.

She rolled her eyes. "Can I trust *anything* you say?"

Alec found himself captivated by the twinkle in her blue irises and the dark lips that contrasted with her creamy skin. She was charming and incredibly kissable, and he had to ruthlessly pull himself back to business.

"Are you aware that Ryder Equine Center has next to no income?" he asked, his blunt tone an admonishment of himself, not her.

When the sparkle vanished from her eyes, he told himself it was for the best.

"We make money," she asserted.

"A drop in the bucket compared to what you spend." Sure, they sold a few horses, boarded a few horses and took in tuition from students. And Stephanie had won some cash prizes in jumping competitions over the years. But the income didn't begin to compare with the massive expenditures necessary to run this kind of operation.

She gestured to the magazine cover. "And there's that."

"Nobody's disputing that you win."

"I mean the marketing value. That's the front cover of *Equine Earth*. It was a four page article. Check out the value of *that* on the open market."

"And how many potential lessees of Chicago office tower space do you suppose read *Equine Earth* magazine?"

"Plenty. Horse jumping is a sport of the rich and famous."

"Have you done an analysis of the demographics of the *Equine Earth* readership?"

Her lips compressed, and she set her coffee mug down on a table.

Alec regretted that she'd stopped smiling, but he forced himself to carry on. "I have no objection to assigning a value to marketing efforts—"

"Well thank you *so* much, oh guru of the framework for overseas economic regions."

"Hey, I'm trying to have a professional—"

The front door cracked sharply as it opened, and Alec instantly clamped his mouth shut. He turned to see Royce appear in the doorway, realizing how loud his and Stephanie's voices had risen.

But Royce's smile was easy, his nod friendly. Obviously they hadn't been overheard.

"Hey, Royce." Stephanie went to her brother, voice tone down, smile back in place.

Royce gave her a quick hug, then he turned his attention to Alec. "Am I interrupting something?"

"We were talking about my career," Stephanie chirped. "The publicity Ryder Equestrian Center brings to the entire corporation." She looked to Alec for confirmation.

He nodded, grateful she seemed willing to keep their spat private.

"Did you show him the video?" Royce asked.

Stephanie looked instantly wary. "He doesn't need to see the video."

Royce set her aside and strode into the room. "Sure he does. What better way to understand your career. Got any popcorn?"

"We haven't had dinner yet. I'm not—"

"Then let's grill some burgers." Royce pushed up the sleeves of his cotton, Western shirt. "I could use a burger. How about you, Alec?"

"Sure. Burgers sound good." So did watching videos of Stephanie, especially since she seemed hesitant. Did she have something to hide?

"Well, I'm not sticking around for this," Stephanie warned.

"Aren't you hungry?" asked Royce.

She stuck her freckled nose in the air. "I'll get something at the cookhouse."

"Suit yourself," said Royce, and Alec caught the faintest glimpse of satisfaction on the man's face.

What was going on here?

Stephanie stuffed her feet into a pair of worn leather boots, shrugged into a chunky gray sweater and stomped out the door.

"I thought she'd never leave," said Royce.

Alec peered at the man. "What's going on?"

Royce turned down the short passage to the kitchen. "We're grilling burgers and watching family videos."

Twenty minutes later, Alec bit into a juicy, flavorful burger. He had to admit, Royce really knew his way around an outdoor grill. Alec was starving, and the burger was fabulous, slathered in fried onions, topped with a thick slice of garden fresh tomato, and encased in what had to be a homemade bun.

Beside him in the opposite armchair, Royce clicked the remote control on the television. "If anyone asks," he said, settling down to his own dinner. "We were simply eating burgers and watching home videos."

Chewing and swallowing, Alec glanced from their plates to the television and back again. "No problem. I've got your back."

Royce nodded.

They made their way through their meals as a young, red-haired Stephanie bounced over foot high jumps on a white pony. Her small hands were tight on the reins, her helmet was slightly askew, and her face was screwed up in determination as she cleared the rails.

Alec couldn't help but smile, and he wondered why Stephanie objected to him watching. She was adorable.

In his short time he'd spent down at the main house on the Ryder Ranch with Royce and his fiancée, Amber, Alec definitely got the sense that both Royce and Stephanie's oldest brother Jared were in the habit of indulging her. Looking at this video, and knowing the age difference between Stephanie and her two brothers, it was easy to see how that had happened.

Turning toward a crisscrossed jump, the pony gathered itself. Stephanie stood in the stirrups, leaning across its neck. The animal's front legs lifted off the ground, back feet kicking out. The pair sailed over the white painted rails, jolting to the dirt on the other side.

The horse came to a halt, but Stephanie kept going, flying over its head, arms flailing as she catapulted forward, thudding into the dirt. Luckily the horse veered to one side, stepping neatly around her little body.

Jared and Royce both ran into the frame. The two teenagers gingerly turned their sister over, talking to her—though Alec couldn't make out the words—brushing the dirt from her little face.

She sat up. Then she nodded, bracing herself on Jared's shoulder and coming to her feet.

Her brothers kept talking, but she shook her head, walking determinedly toward the pony, taking the reins, and circling around to mount. She was too short to put her foot in the stirrup, so Royce gave her a leg up.

Jared kept arguing, looking none too happy. But Stephanie got her way. She turned the horse, heading to the end of the arena. The camera followed her as she restarted the course.

Alec shook his head, his feelings a cross between admiration and amusement.

Suddenly Royce set his plate aside and lifted the remote control, muting the sound.

Alec turned his attention.

"There's something you need to know." Though Royce's tone was even, his expression was narrowed and guarded.

Alec arched a brow.

"This needs to be kept in the strictest confidence," Royce warned.

"Everything you tell me is kept in the strictest confidence." It was a hallmark of Alec's business.

Royce nodded sharply.

Alec waited, his curiosity growing.

"Right," said Royce, fingers drumming against the

leather arm of the chair. He drew a breath. "Here it is then. We're being blackmailed." He paused. "It's Stephanie."

"What did she do?" Dope a horse? Fix a competition?

Royce scowled. "She didn't *do* anything. She's the one in the dark, and we're keeping it that way."

Right. Stupid conclusion. Alec tried another tactic. "Who's blackmailing you?"

"I'd rather not say."

"Okay…" Alec wasn't sure where to go with that.

"It's the biggest drain on the cattle ranch's account."

At least that explained why Amber thought Alec ought to know.

"How much are we talking about?" he asked.

"A hundred thousand a month."

"A *month?*"

Royce's expression was grim as he nodded.

Alec straightened in his armchair. "How long has this been going on?"

"At least a decade."

"*Excuse* me?"

"I know."

"You've spent *twelve million dollars* keeping a secret from Stephanie?"

Royce rocked to his feet, shoulders square, hands balled.

"Must be one hell of a secret."

Royce twisted round to glower at Alec.

"Sorry. None of my business," said Alec.

Still, he couldn't help sifting through the possibilities in his mind. Was there a shady business deal in their past? Did the family fortune originate from an unsavory source? Gambling? Bootlegging?

"You won't figure it out," said Royce.

"I might."

"Not this. And I don't want you snooping around."

"I won't snoop," Alec agreed. He'd respect his client's wishes. "But I might think."

Royce gazed at the silent screen where an elevenish Stephanie was taking yet another spill. "Suppose you can't stop a man from thinking."

"No, you can't."

"Aw, hell." Royce heaved a sigh and sat back down.

Alec gave him a moment. "How bad can it be?"

Royce scoffed out a harsh laugh. "My father was a murderer and my mother was adulterous." He paused. "We're being blackmailed by her lover's brother. The lover was also the murder victim." Another pause, and Royce's voice went lower. "*That's* how bad it can be."

Alec's brain filled in the blank. "And Stephanie is your half sister."

Royce drew back sharply, his expression confirming the truth.

Alec shrugged. "That's the only possibility worth twelve million dollars."

"She's *never* going to know."

"You can't keep paying him forever."

"Oh, yes, we can." Royce grasped the back of his neck. "My grandfather paid until he died. Then McQuestin paid. I took over a couple months ago."

Though it went beyond the bounds of his contract, Alec felt an obligation to be honest. "What are you going to do when he ups his price?"

It was obvious from Royce's expression that he hadn't considered that possibility.

"You'll eventually have to tell her, Royce."

Royce shook his head. "Not if we stop him."

"And how are you planning to accomplish that?"

"I don't know." Royce paused. "Got any ideas?"

Two

Last night's cookhouse burger hadn't measured up to Royce's talents, but it had filled Stephanie's hunger gap. And at least she'd avoided one more screening of *Stephanie Hits the Dirt Across America*.

It was one thing to show that bloopers reel to friends and family, but to strangers? Business associates? She was busy trying to get Alec to take her seriously, and Royce was making her look like a klutz.

Nice guy her brother.

She opened the wooden gate to Rosie-Jo's stall in the center section of the main horse barn and led the mare inside. The vet had given the horse a clean bill of health, and they'd had a great practice session this morning. Rosie had eagerly sailed over every jump.

Stephanie peeled off her leather gloves, removed Rosie's bridle and unclipped the lead rope, reaching through the gate to coil it on the hook outside the stall. She selected a mud brush from the tack box and stroked it over Rosie's withers and barrel, removing the lingering dirt and sweat from the mare's dapple gray coat.

"How'd it go?" Wesley's voice carried through the cavernous barn. His boot heels echoed as he crossed from Rockfire's stall to Rosie-Jo's. He tipped back his Stetson and rested his arms on the top rail of the gate.

"Good," Stephanie answered, continuing the brush strokes.

Though she didn't look up, a shimmer of anticipation tightened her stomach. The barn was mostly empty, the grooms outside with other horses and students. She hadn't talked to Wesley since their aborted kiss two days ago. If he wanted to try again, this would be the opportunity.

"Hesitation's gone," she added. "You tacking up?"

Wesley nodded. "Rockfire's ready to go. Tina has them changing up the jump pattern for us."

Stephanie gave Rosie-Jo's coat a final stroke. Normally she'd do a more thorough job, but she could always come back later. For now, she wanted to give Wesley another chance. Meet him halfway, as it were.

She replaced the brush, dusted her hands off on the back of her blue jeans and started across the stall to where he was leaning over the rail. Suddenly shy, she found she couldn't meet his eyes. Was she being too blatant, too obvious? Should she make it a little harder for him to make his move?

It wasn't like she was experienced at this. Ryder Ranch was a long way off the beaten track. She'd never had a serious romantic relationship, and it had been months— she didn't want to count how many—since she'd even had a date.

She came to a stop, the slated gate a barrier between them. When she dared look at his face, his lips were parted. There was an anticipatory gleam in his blue eyes. And his head began to tilt to one side.

Should she lean in or let him take the lead?

"Am I interrupting anything?" It was Alec's voice all over again, and his footfalls rapped along the corridor floor.

Wesley's hands squeezed down on the gate rail, frustration replacing the anticipation in his eyes.

"Is this some kind of a joke?" he rasped for Stephanie's ears only.

She didn't know what to say. Alec seemed to have a knack for bad timing.

"I'm sorry," she whispered to Wesley.

"Not as sorry as I am."

She turned to face Alec. "Can I *help* you?"

"I hope so." He stopped. After a silent beat, he glanced meaningfully at Wesley.

Wesley glared at him for a moment then smacked his hand down on the rail. "Time for practice," he declared and turned on his heel to lead Rockfire from his stall.

As she watched the pair leave, disappointment clunked like a horseshoe to the bottom of Stephanie's stomach.

"What is it now?" she hissed at Alec, popping the latch and exiting the stall. After securing it behind her, she set off after Wesley.

"Places to go?" asked Alec, falling into step.

"Things to do," she responded, with a toss of her hair. She was going to watch Wesley's practice session. It was part of her job as his coach. Plus, she'd be there when he finished. And by then, Alec should be long gone.

"I'm trying to help you, you know."

"I can tell."

"Is your sex life more important than your company?"

Stephanie increased her pace, stomping forward, ignoring Alec's question.

Sex life.

Ha! She couldn't even get a kiss.

She passed through the open barn doorway, squinting into the bright sunshine, focusing on Wesley who was across the ranch road, mounting Rockfire.

Too late, she heard the roar of the pickup engine, then the sickening grind of tires sliding on gravel.

She had a fleeting glimpse of Amber's horrified face at the wheel before a strong arm clamped around Stephanie's waist and snatched her out of harm's way.

Alec whirled them both, sheltering Stephanie against the barn wall, his body pressed protectively against hers as the truck slid sideways, fishtailing out of control, roaring past to miss them by inches.

"You okay?" his voice rasped through the billowing dust.

She told herself to nod, but her brain was slow in interpreting the signal.

"You okay?" he tried again, louder.

This time, Stephanie managed a nod.

"Stay here," he commanded.

And suddenly, he was gone. Without Alec's physical support, her knees nearly gave way. She grabbed at the wall, mustering her balance, blinking the blur from her eyes while the world moved in slow motion.

As she turned, she took in two ranch hands across the road. Their eyes were wide, mouths gaping. Wesley struggled to control Rockfire, turning the big horse in dust-cloud circles.

Stephanie followed the direction of the hands' attention. A roar filled her ears as Amber's blue truck keeled up on the left wheels.

Alec was rushing toward it

Stephanie tried to scream. She tried to run. But her voice clogged down in her chest, and her legs felt like lead weights.

Then the truck overbalanced, crashing down on the driver's door, spinning in a horrible, grinding circle until it smacked up against an oak tree.

The world zapped back to normal speed. Amongst the cacophony of shouts and motion, Alec skidded to a stop. He peered through the windshield for a split second, then he clambered his way up to the passenger door, high in the air.

He wrenched it open, and Stephanie's body came back to life. She half ran, half staggered down the road, Amber's name pulsing over and over through her brain.

Alec swiftly lowered himself into the truck.

Stephanie grew closer, praying Amber was all right.

Suddenly Alec's sole cracked against the inside of the windshield, popping it out.

"Bring a truck," he shouted, and two of the ranch hands took off running.

Stephanie made it to the scene to see blood dripping down Amber's forehead. The realization that this was all her fault, made her stagger.

Alec met her eyes. "She's okay," he told her, his voice steady and reassuring. "Call Royce. But tell him she's okay."

Stephanie saw that Amber's eyes were open.

She looked dazed, but when Alec spoke to her, Amber answered back.

His hands moved methodically over her body, arms, legs, neck and head.

But then Stephanie saw it.

"Smoke," she tried to shout, but her dry throat wouldn't cooperate.

Alec saw it, too.

People ran for fire extinguishers, while Alec fumbled with Amber's seat belt.

While he worked, he spoke calmly and firmly.

Stephanie couldn't hear the words, but Amber nodded and swallowed. She wrapped her arms around Alec's neck, as the first flames snaked out from under the hood.

He spoke to Amber again, and she closed her eyes, burying her face against Alec's neck. His arms tightened around her, and he slowly, gently eased her through the opening left by the windshield.

Stephanie held her breath, her glance going from the growing flames, to Amber and back again.

Wesley appeared by her side. "You okay?"

The question annoyed her. "I'm fine." It was Amber who was in trouble. And Alec, who might get hurt or worse trying to save her.

The flame leaped higher.

Alec's foot touched the ground outside the truck.

He gripped Amber close to his chest, rising to rush away.

"Get back!" he shouted to the growing crowd, just as the hood blew open, missing the tree trunk and cracking against the roof of the cab.

He staggered forward, but stayed upright and didn't lose his grip on Amber.

Three hands arrived with fire extinguishers, aiming them at the engulfed truck.

Stephanie backed away from the heat. Remembering the cell phone in her hand, she quickly dialed Royce's number.

Another pickup pulled up, and Alec lay Amber carefully across the bench seat.

"Don't try to move," he warned her.

"Hello?" Royce's voice came into Stephanie's phone.

"Royce?" Her voice shook.

"Stephanie?"

She didn't know what to say.

Alec scooped the phone. "Alec here." He took a breath. "There's been an accident. Amber's fine." A pause. "No. No one else was in the truck." He glanced at Stephanie, then down at Amber. "She's conscious."

He moved the phone away from his mouth. "Can you talk to Royce?"

Amber nodded, so Alec handed her the phone. Then he motioned to everyone else to back off. They obeyed, with the exception of Wesley who still hovered next to Stephanie.

When Amber put the phone to her ear and listened, tears welled up in her eyes. Stephanie instinctively moved in to comfort her, but Alec stopped her with his arm.

"Don't touch her," he whispered, keeping his arm braced around Stephanie's waist.

He reached into his pocket, retrieving his own cell phone.

Stephanie looked at him with a question.

"Medical chopper," he said in a low voice, turning away from Amber to speak to emergency services.

Stephanie's attention immediately returned to Amber. Blood was still oozing from the cut on her forehead, and there was a wicked bruise forming on her right shoulder. Her blouse was torn, her knuckles scraped.

Was she really okay? Had Alec lied to Royce? And what did Alec know anyway? He wasn't a doctor.

Okay, so he knew enough to pull Amber from a burning truck.

That was something.

That was huge.

While Stephanie, Stephanie had been stupid enough to march out in front of Amber and cause all this.

Her chest tightened with pain, and a sob escaped from her throat.

Alec turned back. His arm moved from her waist to her shoulders, and he gave her a squeeze. "It's not your fault," he rumbled in her ear.

But his words didn't help.

"Listen to me, Stephanie." He kept his voice low. "Amber is fine. The chopper will be here in fifteen minutes. But it's just a precaution."

"You're not a doctor," she snarled.

"No, I'm not."

"I'm sorry." Stephanie shook her head. "You pulled her out. She could have—"

"Stop."

Amber let the cell phone drop to her chest. "Royce is on his way." Her voice was weak, but just hearing it made Stephanie feel a little better.

"The medical chopper's going to beat him here," Alec told Amber, lifting the phone and gently smoothing her hair away from the wound.

"Want to bet?" Amber smiled, and Stephanie could have wept with joy.

Somebody had located a first aid kit, and Alec gently

cleaned the blood from around Amber's head wound and placed a square of gauze to stop the bleeding.

"Are you okay?" Stephanie dared to ask her.

"Did I hit you?" Amber asked back with a worried frown. "Are you hurt?"

Stephanie quickly shook her head. "No. No. Not at all. I'm perfectly fine. Just worried about you."

"I'm a little stiff," said Amber. She wiggled her fingers and moved her feet. "But everything's still working."

Stephanie mustered a watery smile.

Amber's eyes cut away to focus over Stephanie's shoulder. "I guess that's it for the truck, though."

"It was pretty spectacular," Wesley put in.

Alec frowned at him. "A small fire can do a lot of damage."

Amber looked back at Alec. "Thank you," she told him in a shaky voice.

"I'm just glad you're all right." His smile was so gentle that something warm bloomed to life inside Stephanie.

Amber was going to be okay, and it was because of Alec.

Royce's truck appeared over the rise, tires barely touching down between high spots on the dirt road. A cloud of dust rolled out behind him.

And then he was sliding to a stop at the scene. He burst out of the driver's door, hitting the ground running as the *thump, thump, thump* of the chopper blades sounded in the sky.

Alec watched the towing company employees winch the wrecked pickup onto the flatbed truck. He'd talked to Jared in Chicago, and they agreed to have it removed as quickly as possible. Royce had called to report that Amber would be released from the hospital in a couple of hours. Alec was relieved to learn that Amber's recovery would be short.

She had a few stitches in her forehead, but there were no worries of a concussion. Other than that, she'd only suffered scrapes and bruises. Royce was getting them a hotel room in Missoula, and they were coming home in the morning.

Steel clanked and cables groaned as the half-burned hulk inched its way up the ramps. Several of the ranch employees stood to watch. But it was nearing eight o'clock, and most had returned to their jobs or their homes once they heard the good news about Amber.

Stephanie appeared beside Alec, tucking her cell phone into her pocket and pushing her messy hair back from her forehead. "Amber's making jokes."

Alec was also relieved to see Stephanie getting back to normal. She hadn't been injured, but she'd seemed almost in shock there for a few minutes.

"And how are you doing?" he asked.

"Just a little worn-out." She stilled to gaze at the flatbed that was silhouetted by the final vestiges of a sunset.

"You sure?" he probed.

"I'm sure," she confirmed, voice sounding stronger.

"Good for you."

One of the towing operators was tying down the pickup, while the other started up the engine of the flatbed. Work here was done.

He turned, then waited for Amber to start back to the house with him. Lights had come on in the staff cottages. The scent of freshly cut hay hung in the cooling air. And the diesel truck rumbled away down the ranch road, toward the long hill that wound past the main ranch house to the highway.

"I was looking for a media file," said Alec as the engine faded and the crickets took over.

"A what?"

"That's why I came to find you earlier. Do you have documentation of your jumping career publicity?"

She looked confused.

"I'll need the background information to calculate the dollar value of the exposure," he elaborated.

"I don't understand."

"What's not to understand?"

"You can switch gears that fast?"

It was his turn to draw back in confusion.

"You just risked death to save Amber."

"Risked death?" he chuckled, but then he realized she was serious.

"How did you know how to do that?" she asked.

"It's not exactly rocket science."

She peered at him through the dim glow of the yard lights. "Were you with the fire department or search and rescue?"

"No."

"You pull a woman from a burning truck and carry her to safety only seconds before it explodes. How does that not rattle you?"

"That's the Hollywood version." He steered their course around the corner of the big barn, linking up with the path to her front porch. "I kicked out a windshield. I didn't defuse a nuclear weapon."

"You risked life and limb."

"You know you tend to overdramatize, right?" He did

what needed to be done, and only because he was the closest guy to the wreck.

And, quite frankly, it wasn't fear of the fire and for Amber's safety that had stuck with him. The worst moment had been that split second before he'd pulled Stephanie out of the way of the truck.

"You saved a woman's life, and just like that." She snapped her fingers. "You're working on some mundane report."

"Correction. I'm *trying* to work on a mundane report. Do you maybe have a list or something?"

They'd arrived at the house and mounted the steps, heading in through the door.

Stephanie kicked off her muddy boots, socks and all. "I have a few scrapbooks down at the main house."

"Can we pick them up tomorrow?"

"Sure." She pulled the elastic from her ponytail and ran her fingers through her messy hair. The action highlighted its auburn shimmer, while the pose showed off the compact curves of her body.

It was a struggle not to stare. So, he moved further into the house to where his work was spread out on the dining room table. He dropped into a padded chair, reminding himself of where he'd left off.

"Alec?" she called, coming around the corner.

"Yes?"

When she didn't answer, he couldn't help but turn to look.

She'd stripped off her cotton work shirt and now wore a thin, washed-out T-shirt and a pair of soft blue jeans that hugged her curves. The jeans rode low, revealing a strip of soft, pale skin above the waistband. Her bare feet struck him as incredibly sexy as she padded across the hardwood floor.

"What is it about your past life that led you to rush into a burning vehicle while everybody else stood there and stared in horror?"

"Let it go."

She might look soft and sweet, but the woman had the tenacity of a pit bull.

"I'm curious," she told him.

"And I have work to do."

"It's not a normal thing, you know."

"It's a perfectly normal thing. A dozen guys out there would have done the same."

Stephanie shook her head.

Alec rolled his eyes and turned back to his spreadsheet.

"Let me guess," she carried on. "You were in the marines."

"No."

"The army?"

"Go away."

That surprised a laugh out of her. "It's my house."

"It's my job."

She pondered for a minute. "There's an easy way to get rid of me."

He slid a quizzical gaze her way.

"Answer the question."

He wasn't exactly sure what to say, but if it would get her out of the room and off his wayward mind, he was game to give it a try. "I was in the Boy Scouts."

She frowned. "That's not it."

"Visited dangerous cities?"

A shake of her head.

"Had the occasional bar fight? Never started one," he felt compelled to point out.

She braced her hands on the back of a chair and pinned him with a pointed stare.

"You're not leaving," he noted.

"That's all you've got?" she demanded.

"What more do you want?"

"I don't know. Something out of the ordinary. Something that taught you how to deal with danger."

"I grew up on the south side of Chicago."

"Seriously?"

"No, I'm making that part up."

"Was it in a dangerous part of town?" she asked, leaning forward, looking intrigued.

Alec liked the way her pose tightened her T-shirt against her body.

"Relatively," he told her. Crime had been high. Fights had been frequent. He'd learned how to read people and avoid situations, and how to handle himself when things went bad.

Her voice went low and intimate, as if somebody might overhear them. "Were you like a gang member? In rumbles and things?"

He reflexively leaned closer, lowering his own voice. "No gang. I was raised by a single father, a Chicago cop with very high standards of behavior." Not that Alec had ever been tempted to join a gang. But his father most certainly would have stopped him cold.

"Your father's a police officer?"

Alec sat back. "Not anymore. He's owner and CEO of Creighton Waverley Security."

"So, you work for him?"

Alec shook his head. Work for his old man? Not in

this lifetime. "I do occasional contract work for his company."

"Like this?"

"This is a private arrangement between me and Ryder International."

"There's an edge to your voice."

"That's because you're still asking questions."

"Are you mad at me or your father?"

"Do you ever stop?"

"Do you?"

"I'm paid to ask questions."

"Yeah?" The smile she gave him sent a rush of desire to every pulse point in his body. "I do it recreationally."

They stared at each other in thickening silence, and he could hear the alarm bells warming up deep in the base of his brain. Both Royce and Jared were protective of their sister, and they would not take kindly to Alec making a pass at her.

Not that Alec would ever make a pass at a client.

He never had.

Of course, he'd never wanted to before, either.

So, maybe it wasn't his high ethical standards that kept him on the straight and narrow. Maybe he'd simply never been presented with a client who had creamy skin, deep, cherry lips, perfectly rounded breasts and the wink of a navel that made him want to wrap his arms around her waist, drag her forward and press wet kisses against her stomach until she moaned in surrender.

A sudden rap on the door jolted him back to reality.

It couldn't be Royce. He was still at the hospital. And Jared was in Chicago.

Stephanie hesitated but then turned from Alec and

moved into the alcove off the living room to open the front door.

"I just wanted to make sure you were okay." Wesley's eager voice carried clearly across the room.

Of course.

The soon-to-be boyfriend.

Wasn't that a nice dose of reality.

Three

Brushing her teeth in the en suite bathroom, Stephanie couldn't help but replay Alec's rescue over and over in her mind.

In the moments after the crash, she'd been preoccupied with Amber's safety. And then the helicopter arrived, and the tow truck, and the staff were all anxious and needing to talk. And later she'd been preoccupied with Alec.

But now she knew that Amber was safe. She was alone with her thoughts, and she found herself focusing on those seconds in Alec's arms.

He was surprisingly strong, amazingly fast and obviously agile. His strength had given her a sense of security. Then later, while they'd argued, she'd felt a flare of something that was a whole lot more than security.

She couldn't exactly put a name to it. But it was strong

enough, that when Wesley had showed up, he'd seemed bland by comparison.

She spat the toothpaste into the sink and rinsed her mouth. As she replaced the toothbrush in the charger, she paused, gazing at herself in the mirror.

Attraction, she admitted, glancing at the door that led from the opposite side of the bathroom into the guest room where Alec was sleeping.

She was attracted to him.

She wanted it to be Wesley, but it was Alec.

She gritted her clean teeth, dragged a comb through her curls, braided them tight and snagged an elastic before heading back into her bedroom.

The window was wide, a cool breeze sliding down from the craggy peaks, while the horses blew and snorted in the fields below. Thoughts still on Alec, roving further into forbidden territory, she dropped her robe onto a chair and climbed between the crisp sheets. Her laundry was still behind, and she was prickly warm, so she'd gone with panties and an old tank top, soft as butter against her skin.

She closed her eyes, but nothing happened.

Well, nothing except an image of Alec appearing behind her eyelids.

When he first showed up, he was just a good-looking city guy. There were plenty of those in magazines and on television. And she'd never been particularly attracted to men based on looks alone.

But now she knew his business clothes masked solid muscles. Worse, she'd learned he had a quick mind and a whole lot of courage. And he'd likely saved her life—which was probably a classic aphrodisiac.

Whatever the cause, she could tell she wasn't getting to sleep anytime soon.

She tossed off her comforter, letting the breeze cool her skin, staring out at the three-quarter moon, trying not to think about Alec in the next room. So close.

No. Not so close. So far.

It was fine for her to lay here and fantasize, she told herself. It was perfectly normal and perfectly natural. In real life, it needed to be Wesley, but here in the dark of night…

She flipped onto her stomach. Then she fluffed her pillow and searched for a comfortable position.

She couldn't find one. She flipped back again, reaching for the water glass on her bedside table. It was empty.

Sighing in frustration, she clambered from the bed and crossed the carpet to the bathroom. Opening the door, she flicked on the light.

That exact moment, the door from Alec's room swung open. They both froze under the revealing glare, staring at each other in shock. Her hormones burst to instant attention, and she nearly dropped the glass.

Alec's chest was bare, the top button of his slacks undone. His hair was mussed, and his chin showed the shadow of a beard. As she'd guessed from his embrace, his shoulders were wide, his biceps bulged, and the pecs on his deep chest all but rippled under the light.

His gaze flicked down her body, stopping at her panties, and tension flicked in the corners of his mouth. "Is that from today?"

Her heart pushed hard against her ribs, knowing the skimpy outfit was very revealing.

"Did I *hurt you?*" he demanded.

And then she realized he wasn't salivating over her

bare legs, her skimpy top or the high-cut panties. His gaze had zeroed in on the bruise from where she'd fallen off Rosie-Jo.

She couldn't decide whether to feel relieved or disappointed. "It wasn't you," she assured him. "I fell off my horse."

He took a step forward. "Have you seen a doctor?"

"It's just a bruise."

"It looks deep. Do you need some ice?"

I'm standing here nearly naked. "No."

He moved closer still, and a hitch tightened in a band around her chest, while her hormones raced strategically around her body.

"It'll take the swelling down," he went on. "I can run to the kitchen and—"

"Alec!"

"What?"

"I'm standing here in my underwear."

He blinked. "Right." Then his eyes darkened to charcoal. "Right," he said, his gaze skimming her from head to toe.

She wished she could tell what he was thinking, but his expression gave away nothing. After a long minute, he drew a breath. "Sorry." He took a step back.

"Alec—"

He shook his head, holding up his palms. "Let's just forget this ever happened."

He was right, of course. But she couldn't seem to stop the thick layer of disappointment that slid its way through her stomach. Did he not find her even remotely attractive?

She guessed not, since he hadn't even noticed how she was dressed until she'd pointed it out.

He might have saved her life. He might care about

her physical safety. But apparently it was in a purely platonic way.

"I wasn't—" He took another backward step. "I didn't—" He shook his head. "I'm sorry," he repeated. Then he shot through the doorway to firmly click the door shut behind him.

Stephanie was sorry, too. But she suspected it was for an entirely different reason.

Alec spent the next few days working as fast as humanly possible and avoiding Stephanie as much as he could—which didn't turn out to be difficult, since she was an early riser, and she worked long hours.

Keeping himself from thinking about her proved a considerably tougher challenge. The picture of her in her tank top and panties was permanently seared into his brain stem.

Her face had been scrubbed and shiny, not that she ever seemed to wear makeup. Her shoulders were smooth and lightly tanned, her breasts were perfectly shaped, barely disguised under the thin, white fabric of the well-worn top. Her legs were long and toned, accented by the triangular, flat lace insets of her panties. And her waist was nipped in, stomach flat and smooth.

It had taken all of his willpower not to surge across the tiny bathroom and drag her into his arms.

He drew a shuddering breath, pulled the borrowed ranch truck transmission into fourth gear, and sped up on the final stretch of the road between Stephanie's equestrian stable and the main cattle ranch.

Business Consulting 101, he ruthlessly reminded himself. *Keep your hands off the clients' sister.* His business had been built on integrity. His clients trusted him with sensitive problems that were often high stakes and high risk. If he tossed his principles and made a pass at a client, no one would ever be able to trust him again.

In a self-preservation move, rather than talk to Stephanie face-to-face about her publicity history, he'd mentioned the scrapbooks to Amber. Amber had helpfully offered to hunt them down.

He'd already developed a comprehensive picture of the Ryder Equestrian Center from a business perspective. Not that he was under any illusion that the Ryder brothers wanted to learn the truth about their sister's profitability.

In any event, once he finished with the scrapbooks, he'd head back to the safety of his Chicago office, away from the temptation of Stephanie. The report would stand on its merits. Jared and Royce could use it or ignore it. It was completely up to them.

The main ranch house came into view, and he geared down to control the dust, bringing the truck to a smooth stop on the circular driveway between the house, the barns and the corrals.

Like Stephanie's place, the original ranch house was set on the Windy River. Groves of trees and lush fields stretched out in all directions. There was a row of staff cabins accessed by a small bridge across the river. Working horses were corralled near the house, while clusters of brown and white cattle dotted the nearby hillsides.

Jared Ryder appeared on the porch, coffee cup in hand, and Alec drew a bracing breath as he exited the truck.

He waved a greeting, slammed the door and paced across the driveway. "Didn't know you were in Montana," he said to Jared as he mounted the front steps.

"Just overnight," Jared returned. "Melissa and I wanted to check on Amber."

"How's she doing?"

"She's good. Thanks again, by the way."

"Not a problem."

Despite Stephanie making such a big deal about it, Alec suspected her brothers were both the kind of men who'd rescue anyone in need without a lot of fanfare.

Jared's matter-of-fact nod told Alec he was right.

"I should be done at the Equestrian Center tomorrow," Alec offered. With some hard work, he could wrap things up tonight.

"Glad to hear it. The sooner you get started in Chicago, the better." Then his expression turned serious, voice going lower as he glanced around them. "I hear Royce told you about our little issue."

Alec lowered his own voice in response. "About the blackmail?"

"Yeah."

"He did," Alec confirmed. "And I advised him to come clean with Stephanie."

Jared scoffed out a laugh. "Yeah, that's not going to happen."

"That's exactly what Royce told me."

"He thought you might help?"

"If I can."

Jared gave another considered nod. "Personally, I suggested we hunt him down and—"

"That's not the kind of work I do," Alec quickly put in, on the off chance Jared was serious.

"I wasn't going to suggest we harm him. Though I can't deny the idea has merit. I was thinking more along the lines of explaining to him in excruciating detail what each of us has to gain by ending this, and what each of us has to lose if he keeps it up.

"But it's a moot point anyway. We can't do anything until we find him. And, so far, we haven't been able to find him." Jared gave Alec a significant look.

A moment of silence passed.

"You want me to check into his whereabouts?" asked Alec.

"Amber's friend Katie says you have contacts."

Katie Merrick was a lawyer working for Alec's father's firm, Creighton Waverley Security. Where Creighton Waverley was conservative and by the book outfit, Alec had contacts who could be a little more creative.

"His name is Norman Stanton," Jared offered. "Frank Stanton, Stephanie's biological father, was his brother. The blackmail payments are all tied up in some off-shore company called Sagittarius Eclipse. That's pretty much all we know."

"That's a start." Alec nodded decisively. He'd be more than happy to help track down the man who had targeted Stephanie.

Stephanie needed to purge her wayward fantasies once and for all. And Wesley was the key. Across the arena, he was calling her name, making his way toward her through the soft, deep dirt.

"I've been looking for you," he gasped, as he grew close enough to speak. He ducked through the rails, rising up beside her.

Stephanie was observing Brittany, one of her youngest students, in the starting area of the jumping course.

She smiled briefly at Wesley then nodded to Brittany's trainer, Monica, where she held the bridle of Brittany's horse. Monica stepped back and gave the start signal, and Brittany cantered her horse toward the first two-foot plank.

"How was California?" Stephanie asked Wesley, glancing his way again.

He truly was a fine looking man. His blond hair curled around his ears. He had bright blue eyes and an aristocratic nose. And his quick sense of humor and easy laugh had made him friends throughout the stable.

"It was a long three days," he responded with a warm smile. "My sister has boyfriend trouble. My mother cooked five meals a day. And I missed you."

"I missed you, too." Stephanie told herself it wasn't really a lie, since she wanted so much for it to be true. She rested her elbow on the second rail, tipping her head to look at him.

Truth was she hadn't thought much about him while he was away. Her only excuse was that she'd been busy training. The Brighton competition was coming up in a few short weeks, and it was the unofficial start of qualifying for the Olympic team.

Training was important. It was hard to find time to think about anything else.

Well, except for Alec.

She clamped her jaw down hard, ordering herself to forget about Alec. He'd been skulking around the stable all week, asking questions, printing financial reports, and generally making a nuisance of himself.

Wesley did his part. He took a step closer to her, his shoulder brushing against her elbow.

Brittany turned her horse and headed for jump number four.

Wesley brushed his fingers along Stephanie's bare forearm, easing closer still. He touched the back of her hand, turning it to feather his fingertips across her palm, before cupping her hand and giving her a squeeze.

It was a gentle touch. A pleasant touch. She forced herself to concentrate on enjoying it.

"We need to talk, Stephanie." His blue-eyed gaze went liquid.

"About?"

His smile widened. "About us, of course. I'm dying to kiss you." He moved her hand from the rail and turned her, tugging her toward him, voice going breathy. "I've been thinking about you for three long days."

Stephanie opened her mouth, but the words she wanted to utter wouldn't come out. She hadn't been thinking about Wesley for three long days. And she wasn't dying to kiss him.

Okay, she wasn't exactly opposed to kissing him. But the rush of excitement she'd felt the last two times they'd come close was decidedly absent.

"Tell me how you feel," he breathed.

Brittany cantered past. The clomp of her horse's hooves tossed sprays of dirt, while the *whoosh* of its breathing filled the air. Stephanie used the instant to pull back.

"I really like you, Wesley," she told him.

"That's good." He smiled confidently and moved in again.

"I'm…" Curious? Hopeful? Desperate to have you erase Alec from my thoughts?

"You're what?" he prompted.

"Worried." The word jumped out before she could censor it.

He frowned. "About what?"

"You're my student."

It was a lame excuse, and they both knew it.

Jessica Henderson had been her now husband Carl's student for three years before they announced their engagement. Nobody had been remotely scandalized by the relationship. In fact, half the state horse jumping community had attending their wedding.

"You make me sound like a kid," said Wesley.

"You're younger than me," Stephanie pointed out, feeling suddenly desperate to get out of the kiss she'd been planning for so long.

"Barely," he told her, the hurt obvious in his tone.

"Still—"

"Stephanie, what's going on?"

"Nothing," she lied again.

"I *missed* you."

She tried to come up with something to say.

He stepped into the silence. "You're beautiful, funny, smart—"

"I have a business to run and a competition to train for."

"What are you talking about? What happened while I was gone?"

"Nothing." It was the truth.

His lips puffed out in a pout. "I don't believe you."

Stephanie took a breath and regrouped. "It's just... I need to focus right now, Wesley. And so do you. Brighton is only a few weeks away."

She sped up her words, not giving him a chance to jump back in. "And we both need to nail it. It's your first major, senior event, and I need the ranking."

"I still don't see why we can't—"

"We can't, Wesley."

He reached for her hand once more, squeezing down. "But we're so good together." With the sun slanting across his tousled hair, and the pleading tone in his voice, he suddenly struck her as very young.

"We can be friends," she offered.

His brow furrowed. "I don't want to be friends."

"Yes, you do. We're already friends. We're going to train together and nail Brighton."

"And then what?"

"What do you mean?"

"After Brighton? If we still feel the same way?"

She didn't know what to say. She didn't feel the way she wanted to feel, and she didn't see that changing.

He grinned, obviously taking her silence for agreement. The eager, puppy-dog look was back in his eyes. "I know we have something special."

"We have friendship and mutual respect," she offered carefully.

"There's more than that."

Stephanie took a step back. "Seriously, Wesley, I can't let you—"

"Not right now. I get it." He gave a vigorous nod. "But we both know—"

"No, we don't know—"

Brittany shrieked, and Monica shouted, and Stephanie whirled to see the horse shy to one side. It refused the jump and sent Brittany bouncing into the soft ground.

The girl's breath whooshed out as she landed with a thump on her rear end.

By the time Stephanie was through the fence, Brittany had grabbed two handfuls of dirt and tossed them down in disgust.

She was obviously more angry than injured, but Stephanie rushed to assist just in case.

* * *

Stephanie was angry with herself.

But she was also angry with Alec.

What was he *doing* to her? Why did he have to usurp Wesley? Why couldn't she get the bare-chested image of him out of her head. And *why* hadn't he been interested in her when she was standing half naked in front of him?

All he'd noticed was her stupid bruise.

It was the end of a long, frustrating day, and she marched through the front door. She stripped off her gloves and boots then came around the corner to find the object of her frustration stationed at the dining table, stacks of papers fanned out in front of him. There were magazines, newspaper clippings, financial reports and reference books.

He glanced up, expression unreadable.

She tried to think of a clever greeting, but nothing came to mind. She stood there in silence, her heart beating faster, her hormones revving too high, and her brain tripping up over itself.

"I finished the publicity and promotion calculations," he finally offered. He slid a piece of paper in her direction. "Amber gave me your scrapbooks."

Stephanie ordered her feet to move forward, keeping her attention fixed squarely on the printout as she crossed the hardwood floor. She lifted the paper, scanning to the bottom where each of the past ten years were listed with a corresponding total.

"That can't be right," she found her voice. The numbers were ridiculously low.

"You did get quite a lot of coverage," Alec admitted, setting down his pen and crossing his arms over his chest. "But it's in random placements."

She glanced at him. "Some of those magazines charge tens of thousands of dollars for a single ad. I had the cover. I had the center pages. That's priceless. Ryder International was mentioned over and over again."

"As a targeted placement. Sure, you're going to pay a premium price. But the Ryder International demographic is no more likely to be reading *Equine Earth* as they are to be reading *People* Magazine."

"That's not true."

Alec scraped his chair backward and came to his feet.

"Horse people have money," she repeated her earlier assertion. "They own businesses. They rent real estate."

"Maybe," he agreed. "But maybe not. Now, if Ryder International was in the equestrian equipment business, *Equine Earth*—"

"We're in the equine *breeding* business."

"Revenues from your breeding sales are a tiny fraction of the revenues from the real estate division."

"You're out to get me, aren't you?"

"I'm not—"

She thrust the paper back on the table. "From the minute you walked onto this ranch, you've been out to prove that I'm not a valuable partner in this corporation."

"These numbers aren't my personal opinion—"

"The hell, they're not."

"They're generally recognized calculations for determining—"

"Shut up."

He stiffened. "Excuse me?"

She moved in. "I said shut up. I am so tired—"

"Of what?" he asked incredulously.

"Of you! Of you and your—" She ran out of words. What was she trying to say? That she was tired of being attracted to him? Of knowing that he wasn't attracted to her? Of having his presence at the stable mess with her mind?

He waited, staring hard.

She mustered an explanation. "Of you trying to prove I have no value."

His look turned to confusion. "Is that what you think?"

She gestured to his work with a sweep of her arm. "That's what all this says."

"It says you're a financial drain on the corporation. And you are."

"I'm an asset."

"Not a financial one."

Her throat closed up with emotion, and she hated it.

Why did she care what he thought? Her brothers weren't going to accept this. What could it possibly matter that some opinionated, hired gun of a troubleshooter thought she wasn't pulling her weight?

It shouldn't.

And it didn't.

But then something shifted in his expression, and he cursed under his breath. "I'm trying to be honest, Stephanie."

She didn't trust herself to speak, and she needed him to think it didn't matter, so she waved her hand to tell him to forget about it. She wished he'd back off now and leave her to wallow.

But he took a step closer, then another, and another. His eyes went dark, from pewter to slate to midnight.

She stilled, unable to breathe. Her chest went tight. Her heart worked overtime to pump her thickening blood. And she found herself gazing up at him, feeling the pinpricks of longing flow over her heating skin.

Suddenly he clamped his jaw and his hands curled into fists. "We *can't*."

No, they couldn't.

Wait a minute. Couldn't what? Did he mean what she thought he meant?

"Stephanie. You're my *client*."

Yes, she was.

And that mattered.

At least it should matter.

Shouldn't it?

But a kiss wouldn't hurt. A kiss was nothing. She'd kissed a dozen men, well, boys really. A kiss didn't have to lead anywhere. It didn't have to mean anything.

And then at least she'd know. She'd know his touch, his scent, his taste.

She subconsciously swayed toward him.

"*Stephanie*." His voice was strangled.

The world seemed to pause for breath.

And then he was reaching, pulling, engulfing her, plastering her body against his, flattening her breasts, surrounding her with his strong arms. His mouth came down on hers, open, hot, all encompassing.

Passion shot through her body, igniting every nerve ending, every fiber from her hair to her toes.

He tipped his head, deepening the kiss. She opened her mouth, shocked that these intense sensations could come from a simple kiss. Her arms stretched around his neck, and her body instinctively arched against him.

His hands slid down her spine, lower, and lower still. She gasped at the sensation, moaning when the heat of his palms cupped her bottom.

She curled her fingertips into his hairline, struggling for an anchor, her knees going weak, as the subsonic vibrations of arousal sapped the strength of her legs. She kissed him harder, her thigh relaxing, allowing his own to press between, sending shock waves through her torso.

"Stephanie," he rasped, and she loved the breathless sound of his voice.

He groaned then, breaking away, reaching backward to unclasp her hands.

But she fought back, shaking free from his grasp, cupping his face and peppering his mouth with quick kisses. She did *not* want this feeling to end.

He gave a guttural groan, enveloping her again, taking over the rhythm, bending her backward and thrusting his tongue deep into her mouth while one hand slid up her rib cage, surrounding her breast.

She kissed him fervently, fists tightening, toes curling, as she struggled to get closer and closer.

Then suddenly, she was lifted from the floor, scooped into his arms. The kisses continued and sensations built as he carried her up the stairs to her bedroom. There, he set her down, and his fingers swiftly scrambled with the buttons on her blouse.

Yes. Skin to skin. They absolutely needed to be skin to skin. She fumbled with the knot in his tie, making little progress. She switched to the buttons on his white shirt.

He chuckled deep in his chest as he swooped off her blouse, removing her bra in one deft motion. "I win," he breathed in triumph.

Then he helped her out, and tore open his shirt, discarding it on the floor.

She sighed in sublime satisfaction as his hot body came

up against hers. Her breasts and belly tingled, and her skin flushed with pleasure.

He lifted her once more, sinking onto the bed full-length. His hand found her bare breast, strumming the nipple to exquisite arousal. His kisses roamed from her mouth to her neck to her shoulder, and finally to the hard beads of her sensitized nipples. She was restless, itchy, and her hands felt empty, but she didn't know what to do with them.

She buried them in his short hair, convulsively tightening her fingertips against her scalp. Her thighs twitched apart, and he settled between them. A burst of desire rocketed through her belly. She reached for the waistband of his slacks, certain they needed less clothing between them and more heated skin.

He helped her out again, rising to strip off the rest of their clothes. He paused then, his gaze sweeping hotly over every single inch of her nakedness.

She loved the way he was looking at her, as if he liked what he saw. She loved that she was naked, loved that she could stare right back at his glorious, hot, sculpted body.

He slowly lowered himself against her, one palm running from her knee to her breasts, then back again. He gently eased her legs apart, watching her expression. Then he kissed her eyelids, took her mouth once more in a deep, lingering, passionate kiss.

His touch became firm, his movements more hurried, and when he tore open a condom, she experienced a moment of fear. But then he was back, and his kisses were magic, and her body took over, spreading and arching and welcoming him.

She expected a pain, but it was minor and fleeting, and the building sparks of desire quickly filled her mind. He adjusted her body, and the sensations intensified. She dragged in labored breaths, hands convulsing against his back, toes curled and hips arching to meet him with every stroke.

They rode a wave that stretched on and on, until his body tensed. His rhythm increased. He cried out her name, while lights and sound exploded in her mind, making her weightless, suspended in time, before she pulsed back to earth and felt the weight of Alec on top of her.

His breathing slowed, and he kissed her temple, her ear, her neck.

Then he dragged in a labored gasp. "Stephanie Ryder, you blow my mind."

She struggled to catch her own breath. "If I could talk," she panted. "I'd tell you exactly the same thing."

He chuckled deep, rolling over to put her on top.

Her limbs felt like jelly. But now that it was over, a soreness crept in between her legs. She shifted to ease it.

"Careful," he warned, reaching his hand between them. He eased out of her body.

But then he frowned, lifting his fingers to peer at them in the bright moonlight. "What the hell?"

He whirled his head, pasting her with an accusing look. "You're a virgin?"

"Not anymore."

He recoiled in what looked like horror. "Why didn't you *say something?*"

"Why would I?" It was her problem, not his. Besides, it wasn't like she was saving herself for some mythical future marriage.

"Because…" he sputtered. "Because…"

"Would you have done something different?" Personally she wouldn't have changed a thing. Virginity wasn't a big deal in this day and age.

"I wouldn't have done *anything at all*."

"Liar," she accused. Half an hour ago, neither of them had been thinking past sex. "Did you tell the first woman you slept with that she was the first?"

He frowned in the starlight. "That's completely diff—"

"Ha! Double standard."

He raked a hand through his mussed hair. "I can't believe we're having this argument."

"Neither can I."

"You'll argue about anything, won't you?"

"Takes two to tango, Alec."

He curled an arm around her shoulders and pulled her tight. "You are impossible."

"And you're inflexible."

"You really should have said something." But his voice was starting to fade as a pleasant lethargy took over her body.

"I didn't," she muttered. "Get over it."

His voice dropped to a whisper next to her ear. "I doubt I'll be doing that for a very, very long time."

Her eyes fluttered closed, and her body relaxed into sleep.

Then, after what seemed like only seconds, there was a loud knock on her bedroom door. She blinked, and the bright sunlight stung her eyes.

"Stephanie?" Royce's voice demanded.

Alec was on his feet, clothes in hand, and through the connecting door to the bathroom in a split second.

"Hang on," she shakily called to her brother.

"Something wrong?"

"Why?" She blinked again, struggling to adjust her eyes.

"It's after nine."

She sat straight up and glanced around, grabbing her discarded clothes and stuffing them under the covers just in case Royce barged in. "I overslept."

"Have you seen Alec?"

"Uh, not since last night." Technically, it was true, since she'd had her eyes closed for the past few hours.

"He's not in his room."

The water came on in the bathroom.

"I hear the shower," she called to her brother. "Meet you downstairs?"

There was a pause. "Sure."

Stephanie flopped back down on her pillow, blowing out a sigh of relief. Not that her sex life was any of her brother's business. But, wow. She'd hate to have to listen to the shouting.

Four

As Alec approached the kitchen, he heard both Royce's and Jared's voices. He adjusted his collar, straightened his cuffs and shoved his guilt as far to the back of his mind as humanly possible.

Then he cringed as he passed the messy dining room table. They all would have seen it on their way to the kitchen, and it was completely unprofessional to leave his work scattered like that.

"We're all heading out there in an hour," Jared was saying.

"Good morning," Alec put into the pause, glancing at the faces around the breakfast bar, first at Jared and Royce, then Melissa and Amber, checking for anger or suspicion.

Nothing he could detect, so he allowed himself a quick glance at Stephanie.

Damn it. She looked like she'd made love all night long. And her gaze on him was intense.

When Amber turned toward her, Alec quickly cleared his throat, moving toward the coffeepot, hoping to keep everyone's attention from Stephanie. The woman had no poker face whatsoever.

"Heading where?" he asked Jared as he poured.

"The airport. We can give you a lift."

Alec didn't dare look, but he could feel Stephanie's shock. It wasn't perfect timing, but he couldn't very well refuse the offer after telling Jared he was leaving today. There was work to do in Chicago, and there was also Norman Stanton to deal with.

Besides, what was he going to do if he stayed? Make love to Stephanie again? If they were alone in the same house, odds were good it would happen. His professional ethics were already teetering on the edge of oblivion.

"Thanks," he forced himself to tell Jared. Then he turned, casually taking a sip from the stoneware mug. "Stephanie? I've got a couple more questions before I pack things up." He nodded toward the dining room, hoping she'd get the hint. It might be their one chance to say goodbye alone.

Standing at the opposite side of the breakfast bar, she was blinking at him like a deer in the headlights.

This time Amber did catch Stephanie's expression, and she frowned.

"Stephanie?" he repeated. If she didn't snap out of it, they were going to have one hell of a lot of explaining to do.

"What?" She gave her head a little shake.

"In the dining room? I had a couple of questions."

"Oh. Right." Now she was looking annoyed with him. That was much better.

She followed him out, but Amber came on her heels, followed by Royce and the rest of the family. Alec was stuck with asking Stephanie some inane business questions, to which he already had answers, as he packed the papers away in his briefcase.

In no time, they were heading out the door to Jared's SUV. Alec hung back, but he only managed the briefest of goodbyes and apologies to Stephanie before he had to leave.

Stephanie spent the next few weeks training hard with Rosie-Jo for the Brighton competition. At first, she'd been angry with Alec for his abrupt departure. Then she'd been grateful. After all, there was no sense in prolonging it.

They'd had a one-night stand, no big deal. She couldn't have asked for a better lover. And, though it was short, it had been wonderful, physically, at least.

But then the gratitude wore off, and she felt inexplicably sad and lonely. She found herself remembering details about him—the sound of his laugh, how his gray eyes twinkled when he teased her, his confident stride, his gentle touch, the heat of his lips and the taste of his skin.

She knew she was pining away for something that couldn't be, for something that had never existed in the first place, except in her own imagination.

She didn't think she felt guilty about making love to him. But maybe she did. Maybe that was why she was pretending their relationship was something more than a fling.

Cold fact was, she'd given her virginity to a man she didn't love, a man who was little more than a stranger.

It was the end of another long training day. She stabled Rosie-Jo and double-checked the feeding schedule. Leading up to Brighton, everything about Rosie's regime had to be perfect, as did Stephanie's.

She pressed her hands against the small of her back, arching as she sighed. Her period was a few days late, and she was getting frustrated with the wait. It was only a small difference, but competing at the most favorable hormonal point in her cycle could be the edge she needed to win. If she didn't get it by the weekend, she could be jumping with PMS.

She pulled her ponytail loose, finger-combed her hair and refastened the rubber band as she made her way to the barn door. She was exhausted, almost dizzy with fatigue today. And she was famished.

She took that as a good sign. It wasn't uncommon for her to polish off a pint of ice cream and a bag of potato chips the day before her period started. Not that she'd indulge in either this close to a competition. She'd have some grilled chicken and a big salad instead.

The thought of the food had her picking up her pace across the yard. But by the time she got to the front porch, she'd changed her mind. Chicken didn't really appeal to her. Maybe she'd do a steak instead.

Then she opened the door and caught the aroma of one of her housekeeper Rosalind's stews. She gripped the door frame for a split second. Okay, definitely not stew. She'd sit out on the back veranda and grill that steak.

The next morning, Stephanie blinked open her eyes, surprised to find it was nine-fifteen. The training schedule was obviously wearing her out. Fair enough. Her body was telling her something. She'd make sure she incorporated an extra hour sleep in her routine for the next two weeks.

She sat up quickly, and a wave of nausea had her dropping right back down on the pillow.

Damn it. She could not get sick.

Not now.

She absolutely refused to let a flu bug ruin the competition.

She gritted her teeth, sitting up more slowly. There. That was better. Wasn't it?

She gripped the brass post of her bed, willing her stomach to calm down.

It wasn't fair. First her period screwup, and now this. She needed to do well at Brighton. She'd trained her entire life for this year of all years. But it was as if the stars were lining up against her.

She started for the en suite, telling herself it was mind over matter. She was young and healthy. And she had a strong immune system. She was confident she'd quickly fight off whatever it was she'd picked up.

She stopped in front of the sink, pushing her messy hair back from her face, groping for her toothbrush and unscrewing the toothpaste cap.

She caught a glimpse of herself in the mirror. Her face was pale. Her eyes looked too big today, and the smell of the toothpaste had her rushing to retch into the toilet.

There was little in her stomach, but she immediately felt better. What the heck was wrong—

She froze.

"No." The hoarse exclamation was torn from her.

Her hand tightened on the counter edge and she shook her head in denial. She could *not* be pregnant.

They'd only done it once. And they'd used a condom.

Okay. She breathed. She had to calm down. She was only scaring herself. How many crazy thoughts had popped into her head since Alec left? This was simply one more in the series.

She drew another deep breath. The nausea had subsided.

It had to be psychosomatic. Her period would start today, maybe tomorrow. Her hormones would get back on track. She'd stick to her training regime, and she'd kick butt in Brighton.

Anything else was unthinkable.

On morning four of the nausea and exhaustion, Stephanie dragged her feet to the bathroom, staring with dread at the home pregnancy test she'd picked up the afternoon before. Even before she followed the directions, she knew what the answer would show.

Sure enough, the two blue stripes were vivid in the center of the viewing window. She was pregnant.

She plunked the plastic stick in the trash bin and moved woodenly to the shower.

As the warm water cascaded over her body, she let a tear escape from her eye. Then another, and another.

What oh *what* had she done? This was her year, first the nationals, then the European championships and finally tryouts for the Olympic team.

The moment she'd trained for, longed for, prayed for her entire life was upon her, and she was going to have a baby instead, without a father. Her brothers would be furious on both counts. They'd be so disappointed in her.

Her mind searched hopelessly for a way to keep it secret.

Maybe she could fake an injury and take herself out of competition. Then she would find an excuse to stay in Europe for six months. And, then… And, then…

She whacked the end of her fist against the shower wall in frustration.

What would she do? Come back to Montana with a baby in tow? Tell them she adopted some poor orphan in Romania?

It was a stupid plan.

Defeated, she slowly slid her way down the wall, water drizzling over her as she came to rest on the bottom of the tub. She wrapped her arms around her knees, staring blankly into space as the water turned from hot to tepid.

"Stephanie?" Amber's voice surprised her. It was followed by a rap on the bathroom door.

"Just a sec," Stephanie called out, rising to her feet, swiftly spinning off the now-cold water.

"You okay?" Amber asked.

"Fine." Stephanie flipped back the curtain and grabbed a towel, scrubbing it over her puffy cheeks and burning eyes.

What was Amber doing in Montana?

"You've been in there forever," Amber called.

"What are you doing here?"

"Royce got restless in Chicago. It was either this or fly to Dubai for the weekend. You want to come down to the main house for a while?"

Stephanie pressed her fingertips into her temples. The last thing in the world she needed was one of her brothers hanging around. She needed to be alone right now.

"I have to train," she called through the door.

"You decent?" asked Amber.

"I'm—"

The door opened, and Stephanie quickly wrapped the big bath towel around her body.

"Morning." Amber grinned.

"You never heard of privacy?"

"We're practically sisters." Then Amber's grin faded. She cocked her head, staring into Stephanie's eyes. "What on earth?"

Stephanie quickly turned away, coming face-to-face with her own reflection in the mirror. Her eyes were bloodshot. Her cheeks had high, bright pink spots, but the rest of her face was unnaturally pale.

"I had a rough night," she tried, but her voice caught on her raw throat.

Amber's arm was instantly around her shoulders. "What's wrong? Did you get bad news? One of the horses?"

"No." Stephanie shook her head.

Then Amber's gaze caught on something. Her eyes went wide, and her jaw dropped open.

Stephanie looked down to see the home pregnancy test box on the counter.

"You can't tell Royce," she croaked.

"You're *pregnant*."

Stephanie couldn't answer. She closed her eyes to block out the terrible truth.

"Is it Wesley?"

Stephanie quickly shook her head.

"Who—"

"It doesn't matter."

There was a silent pause, then Amber touched her shoulder. "Alec."

Stephanie's eyes flew open. "You can't tell Royce."

"Oh, sweetheart." Amber pulled Stephanie into her arms. "It's going to be okay. I promise you, it's going to be okay."

It wasn't often that Alec spent time in his Chicago office. For one thing, his jobs rarely kept him in the city.

He preferred to be on the ground, gathering information from real people in different places around the world.

Consequently his office was stark, almost sterile. In a central location between the river and the pier, it was a single room on the thirty-second floor. The view was spectacular. The desk was smoke glass and metal, with sleek curves and clean lines. Matching chairs were thinly padded with charcoal leather. He used his laptop everywhere he went, and his file cabinets were stainless steel, recessed into the wall.

There was no need for a receptionist, since his phone number wasn't published. He wasn't listed on the building's lobby directory, and he rarely had more than one job on the go at a time.

So, it was a surprise when the office door swung open.

Alec glanced up to see Jared fill the doorway. He walked determinedly inside, followed closely by Royce, their faces grim.

They shut the door and positioned themselves on either side, folding their arms across their chests, as Alec came to his feet. There wasn't a doubt in his mind that they knew he'd taken Stephanie's virginity.

"Stephanie told you," he stated the obvious. He wouldn't lie, and he wouldn't deny it. If they fired him, they fired him.

Jared spoke. "Stephanie doesn't know we're here."

Alec nodded and came out from behind the desk, ready to face them.

Royce stepped in. "Stephanie's pregnant."

The words stopped Alec cold.

Seconds dripped like icicles inside the room.

"I had no idea," he finally said.

"You're not denying you're the father," Jared stated.

"I'm not denying anything. Whatever Stephanie told you, you can take as true."

"Stephanie didn't tell us anything," said Royce.

Then Alec wasn't about to add to their body of knowledge. What happened between him and Stephanie was private.

She was pregnant, and he'd absolutely do the right thing. And her brothers had every right to call him on it. But they didn't have a right to anything more than she was willing to voluntarily share.

Jared took a step forward, and Alec wondered if he was going to take a swing.

"Here's what we're going to do," Jared said.

"I *will* marry her," Alec offered up-front.

"Not good enough," said Royce, squaring his shoulders to form an impenetrable wall next to his brother.

Alec didn't understand. There were limited options at this point.

"We don't want to see Stephanie get hurt," said Jared.

Alec's mental reflex was to make a joke about that being the understatement of the century. But he held his tongue.

"No woman wants a marriage of convenience," said Royce.

Alec still wasn't following.

"She wants a love match."

Alec peered at Royce. "Are you saying you want her to marry someone else?" His thoughts went to Wesley, and he found his anger flaring. Wesley wasn't the father of her child. *Alec* was the father of her child.

His mind wanted to delve into that unfathomable concept, but he forced himself to focus on Jared and Royce.

"We mean a love match with you."

Alec gave his head a little shake.

He'd step up. He'd provide financial and any other support needed, but he and Stephanie barely knew each other. They weren't going to settle down and live happily ever after just because her brothers decreed it.

He would never put any woman in that position. He knew from the catastrophe of his own parents' marriage, exactly what happened when you tried to fake it.

"I hope that was a joke," he intoned.

Jared took yet another step forward. "There is nothing remotely funny about any of this."

Alec looked into the man's eyes. "No, there's not. But you can't control people's emotions. She's no more in love with me than I am with her."

"You can change that," said Royce. "Tell her you love her, and make her fall in love with you."

Alec slid his glance sideways. "No."

Not a chance in hell. There was not a freaking chance in hell he would set Stephanie up for that kind of heartache.

Royce squared his shoulders. "It wasn't a question."

Alec could well imagine that few people said no to the Ryder brothers. They were intellectually and physically powerful men. Add to that their economic wherewithal, and they were pretty much going to get their own way in life.

But Alec didn't intimidate easily, and he had a set of personal principles that stopped well short of duping a woman into falling in love with him.

"I'll marry Stephanie," he told them both. "I'll respect her. I will provide for our child. And I'll lie to the world about it if she wants me to. But I won't lie to her."

He gave a harsh laugh. "You two might think you're protecting her by—"

"We *are* protecting her," said Royce, and Jared's expression backed him up.

"Nevertheless," Alec articulated carefully. "*I'm* going to be honest with her."

Since Alec spent most of his life on the road, a marriage of convenience would be fairly easy to pull off. And after the baby was born, she could decide what she wanted. If it was a quiet divorce, no problem.

Jared and Royce glanced uncertainly at each other. It was obvious the meeting wasn't going the way they'd planned.

"May I assume I'm fired?" Alec put in.

The two men exchanged another glance.

Royce cleared his throat.

"I think we'll leave that up to Stephanie," said Jared.

This time Alec did laugh. "Then you might as well take your files with you when you go. She's pretty ticked off about my valuation of her publicity."

The two men hesitated again.

"It is right?" asked Jared.

"It's right," Alec confirmed.

"Let's maybe leave the business arrangement as is for now," said Royce.

Alec glanced from one man to the other. "You sure?"

They both nodded.

"No point in disrupting everything at once," said Jared. Then he clapped a hand down on Alec's shoulder. "You can come back to the ranch with us."

"You afraid I'm going to try to run off?"

"We don't want Stephanie to be upset any longer than necessary."

"She'll still be upset after I get there." Alec tried to picture their conversation. Then he wondered how Stephanie felt about the baby. Then, finally, he let his mind explore how he felt about the baby.

He'd never planned to have children. The genetics in his family did not lend themselves to quality parenting. His father was incapable of love, and his mother had been unable to put her child's welfare ahead of her own misery.

At least Alec's child would have Stephanie.

For some reason, the thought warmed him. Stephanie might be indulged and impulsive, but she was also sweet and loving. He'd seen her work with both animals and children, and he knew instinctively she'd be a great mother.

And he was going to be a father.

As he exited the office with Jared and Royce, he tried hard to keep the prospect from terrifying him.

At the front of the stall, Stephanie rested her forehead against Rosie-Jo's soft nose. She placed her hand on the horse's neck, feeling it twitch and pulse with strength beneath her fingertips.

"I went to see the doctor today," she told Rosie-Jo, wrapping her hands around the mare's bridle.

Rosie-Jo nickered softly in response, bobbing her head up and down.

Stephanie slowly drew back, gazing into the horse's liquid, brown eyes. Her throat closed over. "I'm definitely pregnant, girl."

Rosie-Jo blinked her lashes.

"And that affects you," Stephanie forced herself to continue. "Because he's afraid I might fall off. He's afraid

I'll hurt the baby." Stephanie closed her eyes and drew a bracing breath. "I'm so sorry, Rosie. I know how you love the crowds. And you've worked so hard. And I've worked so hard. For so long."

Rosie snuffled Stephanie's shoulder.

Stephanie opened her eyes to the blur of gray horse hair, her voice catching. "So, he doesn't want me to jump anymore."

"That sounds like good advice to me," someone rumbled behind her.

Rosie snorted, while Stephanie startled. She turned and came face-to-face with the man who'd haunted her dreams.

"Alec?" She struggled to make sense of his presence in the barn. "What are you doing here?"

"Your brothers picked me up in Chicago." His gaze scanned her thin cotton shirt, blue jeans and worn boots.

The implication of his arrival, and the meaning of his opening words penetrated Stephanie's brain.

He knew she was pregnant.

And her brothers must know, too.

She felt the walls close in. She hadn't prepared for this moment, hadn't had any time to even think about it. She'd assumed it would be weeks, even months before her pregnancy was general knowledge.

"I believe Amber gave you up," Alec offered.

Stephanie didn't respond, her mind still grappling with the fact that he knew, that he was here, that the secret was out.

"When were you planning to tell me?" he asked, face impassive, tone guarding his mood.

The word *never* sprang to mind. Though she knew she wouldn't have kept it from him.

"I don't know," she managed, answering him honestly. "I hadn't thought about it." It was enough of a challenge coming to terms with the situation herself.

He shook his head and gave a scoff of disbelief. "You hadn't *thought about it?* You're unexpectedly pregnant, and it's not on your mind twenty-four seven?"

"I just found out."

"You told Amber a week ago."

"And I saw the doctor this morning. I hadn't even decided—"

"Decided *what?*" His voice went deadly low, and his gray eyes turned to black.

"What to do." She had her riding career, her students, her business. Not to mention a baby, then a child. She'd never even known her own mother, how would she handle it all?

He wrapped his hand firmly around her upper arm. "Stephanie, if you even think about—"

She blinked up at him.

"—harming our baby."

Harming? What was he talking...

Then her eyes went wide, and she jerked her arm from his grip. "What is the *matter* with you?"

"Me? You're the one who hasn't made up her mind—"

"How to *raise* the baby." She smacked him on the front of his shoulder. "Not whether to keep the baby."

He didn't even react to the blow. "You can't be happy about this."

"Of course I'm not happy about this. I'm not ready to be a mother. I have a business to run. My jumping career is ruined. And my brothers know I slept with you."

"Your brothers will get over it."

Her brothers. She groaned inwardly.

Royce and Jared knew Alec had made her pregnant.

Wait a minute. She looked him up and down. "You're still standing."

"I am."

She cocked her head. "How come you're still standing?"

"You thought your brothers would kill me for sleeping with you?"

"I never thought my brothers would find out."

"Yeah." He glanced away. "I was kind of counting on the same thing."

Then the fog lifted, and a picture came clear in her mind. Of *course* her brothers hadn't harmed him. They needed him alive.

She didn't know whether to be furious or mortified. "You're here for a shotgun wedding."

"Something like that," he admitted.

She felt guilty on a whole new front now. Alec was a decent guy. He didn't deserve this.

She shook her head. "Don't worry about it."

"Do I look worried?"

"You definitely look worried."

"It doesn't have to be a big deal."

"It doesn't have to be anything at all." Making up her mind, she turned decisively and started down the corridor.

Alec settled in beside her.

She finger-combed her hair and refastened her ponytail at the base of her neck. "Thanks for stopping by, Alec. You're an honorable man. But your baby is safe in my hands. I'll drop you a line once it's born."

He coughed out a laugh. "Yeah, right."

"Your life is in Chicago. Leave this to me." In this day and age, a reluctant husband was a complication not a benefit. What had her brothers been thinking?

"Not quite the way things are going to happen," he said.

"They can't make you marry me."

"Now that part's debatable."

"Okay. Maybe they can make you. But they can't make me." She spotted a length of binder twine on the floor and reflexively stooped to pick it up.

"They want what's best for you, Stephanie."

She wrapped the orange twine neatly around her hand. "No, Alec. They want you to pay for your sins."

"They want to protect you."

She gave a dry chuckle. "From what? A scarlet letter?"

He didn't respond.

"I'm a big girl, Alec. I made a mistake, and I'm going to pay. But it doesn't mean you have to get dragged along for the ride." She peeled the loop of twine from her hand and reached for the door latch.

His hand shot out, blocking the door shut. He stared down at her with an intense singularity of purpose. "Get this straight in your mind, Stephanie. You *are* marrying me."

She squinted at him in the dim light. "That was a joke, right?"

"Am I laughing?"

"I don't know what they threatened you with."

"Nobody threatened me with anything."

"Then why are you talking crazy?"

"I'm talking logic. It doesn't have to be forever."

"And what girl doesn't want to hear *that* in a marriage proposal?"

"Stephanie."

His words shouldn't have the power to hurt her. She barely knew the man. And she needed to keep it that way.

She stuffed the twine in her pocket and crossed her arms over her chest. "Marriage would make a bad situation worse."

He imitated her posture, crossing his own arms. "Marriage would make things right."

Suddenly the entire conversation seemed absurd, and a cold laugh burst out of her. "How do you figure?"

His jaw clenched. "I'm the baby's father."

"Yes?"

"I have a responsibility."

"To do what?"

"I don't know," he practically shouted. "Provide for it."

"You can write a check without having a marriage license."

"Is that what you want?"

"Yes."

"And I have no say?"

"Not really."

He glared at her for a long moment. Then he smacked the door open and marched out of the barn.

As she watched his retreating back, Stephanie realized she had won.

She tried to feel glad about that, but somehow the emotion wouldn't come.

Five

"Well, what was I *supposed* to say?" Stephanie challenged. Sitting on a submerged ledge, water to her waist in the ranch swimming hole, she stared at Amber over the rippled surface of the water.

"Yes?" Amber suggested as she pulled the last couple of strokes across the small, cliff bordered pool and settled on the ledge next to Stephanie. Her forehead was completely healed, and the cut from the accident would barely leave a scar.

The swimming hole was a favorite place for Stephanie. Water from a small tributary to the Windy River trickled down a waterfall and gathered in a deep pool, hollowed out over millennia. The semicircle cliffs were open to the east, so the morning sun soaked into the granite, heating the water, keeping it comfortable all summer long.

It was near noon, and the sun streamed down on Amber's wet, blond hair, reflecting in her jewel-blue eyes.

"And actually *marry* him?" Stephanie swiped her own wet hair back from her forehead, tucking it behind her ears.

"You are having his baby."

"And, we're practically strangers."

"Not completely." Amber's eyes took on a meaningful gleam.

Stephanie glared in return. "Nobody gets married because of a baby anymore."

Amber didn't answer, but an opposing opinion all but oozed from her pores.

"What?" Stephanie prompted.

"You're pregnant, Steph."

"I know that." Stephanie had tried hard to push it from her mind. But the reality wasn't going anywhere.

"A husband might not be such a bad thing."

"I thought you'd be on my side."

"I *am* on your side."

Stephanie snorted her disbelief.

"We're only suggesting you give it a try."

"And if I fail?" Which was a foregone conclusion in Stephanie's mind. And therefore the entire exercise was a waste of time.

"Then you fail. Nothing ventured—"

"We're talking *marriage,* Amber." Stephanie couldn't believe her future sister-in-law could be so cavalier about something so serious. Maybe Stephanie was a hopeless romantic, but she didn't want to stand up in front of God and her family and take vows she didn't mean.

"It doesn't have to be a traditional marriage."

"Maybe that's what I want."

Amber cocked her head, silent for a few moments. "Are you saying you have feelings for Alec?"

"No!" Stephanie's denial was quick. Her emotions caught up a split second later. She didn't have feelings for Alec. She wouldn't allow herself to have feelings for Alec. "I just want…"

"What?"

"Normal. I want something about this entire mess to be normal."

"Define normal." Now Amber was being deliberately obtuse.

"A date? A candlelight dinner? Maybe a movie? Something, anything even a little bit romantic."

Amber snorted out a laugh. "What's romantic? Melissa went undercover and spied on Jared, and Royce picked me up in a bar." She snapped off a twig and tossed it into the pond. "I was a one-night stand that never went home."

Despite herself, Stephanie's interest was piqued. "You and Royce had a one-night stand?"

"Not the first night."

"Which night?"

"None of your business."

"Did you know you loved him?"

"Not at the time."

"Were you a virgin?"

"No."

"But you loved him later. So, somewhere, deep down inside, you must have known."

"Don't do this, Stephanie."

Stephanie clamped her jaw. Amber was right. Comparing herself to Melissa and Amber was futile. They were with men that they loved, men who would stick around, share their lives forever.

Leaves crackled on the trail behind them, and Stephanie turned to see Alec emerge from the trees.

His attention was fixed on Stephanie. "Royce told me I'd find you here."

Amber made to stand up, but Stephanie grabbed at her arm. "Don't go."

"You two have a lot to talk about."

"We've already talked." Stephanie had no desire for a repeat argument. She didn't have the energy.

Amber glanced up, obviously assessing Alec's expression. "I don't think you're done yet." She came to her feet, stepping her way out of the pool where she snagged a towel from a rock. Then she stuffed her feet into a pair of bright blue thongs.

Stephanie braced herself as Alec crouched down beside her. He was wearing a pair of lightweight khakis and plain, white dress shirt. His shoes were too formal, but at least he'd forgone the tie.

"Swimming?" he asked conversationally.

"No. Riding a bike."

"You think sarcasm's going to help?"

"I don't think anything's going to help."

"Right." He shifted. "So, your long-term plan is to wallow in self-pity?"

Stephanie refused to answer. Instead she swung her legs back and forth in the water.

She heard a rustle, then he stepped onto the ledge to sit. He'd stripped down to a pair of black boxers, and she quickly shifted her gaze to the other direction.

"You've seen me naked," he rumbled, amusement clear in his tone.

She might have seen him that way once, but she didn't

intend to see him that way again. She scrambled to put her feet under her.

His hand came down on her shoulder. "Oh, no you're not."

"You're going to hold me prisoner?"

"If I have to." The hand remained firmly in place.

Stephanie gave an angry sigh.

"I was thinking a garden wedding would be nice."

"What part of no didn't you—"

"We could do it here, if you like. Or in Chicago."

"Alec, we can't—"

"There's a ring in my pocket. Simple, but a couple of carats. It should impress your friends." He glanced across the shiny surface of the pool. "Probably not a good idea to give it to you here."

Despite herself, she turned to look at him. "You bought me a diamond?"

"Of course I bought you a diamond. We're getting married."

"You can't bribe me with jewelry, Alec."

"I'm bribing you with a name for our baby."

"I'm hardly a fallen woman."

"This isn't about you, Stephanie."

"Of course it's about—" She almost said me, but she clamped down her jaw instead. Her jumping career was ruined, and that was that. The baby was her priority now.

He smiled. "Ah. A glimmer of responsibility."

"Of course I'll do what's best for the baby." Beneath the water, her hand moved subconsciously to her abdomen.

"Marrying me is best for the baby."

She didn't answer.

"I'm under no illusions that we can 'make it work,'" Alec continued.

"Ah. A glimmer of reality," she mocked.

He frowned at her. "We barely know each other."

"You got that right."

"This isn't my first choice, either."

She stifled a cold laugh, but he ignored her silent sarcasm.

"I'll be honest with you, Stephanie. When it comes to women, I'm not a long-term kind of guy. And I don't see that changing."

Wow. This proposal just kept getting better and better.

Did he mean he'd continue dating? She supposed there was nothing to stop him from doing just that. He had an apartment in Chicago, and he traveled on business most of the time.

She shouldn't care. She had no right to care. Though it would be embarrassing if he was seen in public by someone she knew.

"Will you be discreet?" she asked him.

"Excuse me?"

"With the other women. Will you be discreet?"

His brows knit together. "What other women?"

"You just said your lifestyle wouldn't change."

"I didn't—"

"I assume that means I'm free to see other men," she added defiantly. "Although it would be more complicated for me to—"

"Whoa," he roared. "You are *not* going to be seeing other men."

"Isn't that a double standard?"

"Double *standard?*"

"I'm trying to understand how this will work."

Perhaps refusing Alec had been the wrong strategy. Maybe agreeing to marry him and pressing on the details would be more effective. She'd bet it wouldn't take him long to back out.

"Well, one way it will work, is that my pregnant wife won't be sleeping with other men."

"So, I'll be celibate then?"

"Damn straight."

"For how long?"

"For as long as it takes. It worked just fine for the first twenty-two years of your life."

"That was before."

"Before what?"

Frustration goaded her. "Before I knew how much fun it was to have sex."

Alec's eyes frosted to pewter. His mouth opened then closed again in a grim line.

She didn't care. Let him think she was embarking on a spree of debauchery. So long as it changed his mind about the wedding.

"You're lying," he finally said.

"That sex is fun?" she deliberately misunderstood, crossing her arms beneath her breasts. "You were there, Alec. Do you think I'm lying?"

"You are impossible." But his gaze dipped to her cleavage and the clingy one-piece bathing suit.

The heated look brought a rush of memories, and she realized that talking about their sex life might not be the brightest move. It had been far better than mere fun. And the experience was still fresh in her mind. And, given different circumstances, she'd definitely be in favor of repeating it.

"I'm merely pointing out some of the impracticalities of your master plan," she told him.

"Stephanie, in five or six years, you are going to have a

child in your life asking about their family. Do you want to tell them Daddy was a one-night stand, or do you want to tell them Mommy and Daddy had a fight and don't live together anymore."

Stephanie's brain stumbled on the picture of a five-year-old. There *would* be a five-year-old. And she'd be solely responsible for raising him or her.

Panic rose inside her. How would she manage? Her only role models were a grandfather and two teenage boys.

"I can't—" She came to her feet, water rushing down her legs and dripping from her suit.

Alec rose. "Don't you dare—" But then her expression seemed to register. "Stephanie?"

She was going to have a baby. She was honest to God, going to have a baby.

She felt the blood drain from her face.

She'd never fed a baby, burped a baby, changed a diaper. What if she did something wrong? What if she forgot something important? What if she inadvertently harmed the poor, little thing?

"Stephanie," he sighed in obvious exasperation. He reached for her, pulling her to his body. His bare chest was warm from the sun, and his arms were strong around her. She had a sudden urge to bury her face and hide there forever. His deep voice vibrated reassuringly in her ear.

"Marry me, Stephanie. It won't be perfect. It won't be romantic. But we'll at least be honest with each other."

His sincerity touched her and, miraculously, she didn't feel so completely alone. She let herself sink into Alec's strength. Then she gave in and nodded against his chest.

Stephanie had preferred to hold the wedding at the ranch, and that was fine with Alec. He'd done his duty and informed his father, omitting the fact that Stephanie was pregnant. History might be repeating itself on one level, but the unplanned pregnancy was the only thing his marriage would have in common with his parents'.

Jared and Melissa had flown to the ranch. Then Melissa and Amber had joined forces to convince Stephanie to put on at least a cursory show for the ceremony. It would only be the six of them and a preacher, but they couldn't completely hide the event from the ranch workers, nor should they. It was better if it looked natural.

In the end, they'd chosen a quiet spot by the river. It was a couple of miles up a rutted, grassy road from Stephanie's house, out of sight from the working areas. A field of oats rippled behind them, while horses grazed on the hillside, and the river burbled against a backdrop of cottonwood trees.

Alec and the preacher arrived first, but within minutes, Jared's SUV pulled up with the rest of the party. The men all wore suits, while Amber and Melissa chose knee-length dresses, Amber in bronze, and Melissa in burgundy.

Stephanie was the last to emerge from the backseat. But when she did, Alec couldn't stop staring.

Her white dress was simple, strapless with a high waist and a sparkling belt below her breasts. The skirt fell softly to her knees, showing the curves of her slim, tanned calves. Her shoes were pretty, white satin ballet slippers against the long green grass.

Her hair was upswept, brilliant auburn under the deep, blue sky. She wore diamond earrings and a delicate, matching necklace, and subtle makeup had toned her freckles to nothing. His gaze was drawn to her graceful neck and smooth, bare shoulders.

Alec was far from a romantic man, but he was forced

to fight the urge to sweep her up in his arms and carry her off on a honeymoon.

She took a tentative step forward, and then another.

It was no traditional march down the aisle, and she seemed uncertain of what to do.

Alec moved forward, meeting her halfway, taking her hand so that they approached the preacher together. Her fingertips trembled ever so slightly against his skin, and he fought a thickness in his chest and the desire to pull her tight against him and reassure her. His reaction was ridiculous. The ceremony was as simple as they could make it. They were here to get the job done, nothing more.

The preacher began speaking, and everyone went still.

Stephanie stared determinedly at Alec's chin while she spoke her vows.

Alec by contrast watched her straight on, continuing to marvel at how stunning she looked. He realized that he'd never seen her in a dress, never seen her in jewelry, or with her hair in such a feminine style.

He'd known she was beautiful. He'd been physically attracted to her from minute one. But this incredible creature standing in front of him surpassed any dream or expectation he'd ever had. Once again, he found his imagination moving to a wedding night and honeymoon.

He ruthlessly shut that thought down. He had to keep a distance between them. Royce and Jared's plan to make her fall in love was both foolish and dangerous. Alec's mother had loved his father, and his father's indifference had destroyed her.

Then the preacher was finishing, inviting Alec to kiss the bride.

It seemed silly to do it, but churlish to skip.

So Alec bent his head. He struggled for emotional

distance as he rested a hand on her perfect shoulder, slid the other arm around her slim waist and touched his lips to hers.

It was a tender kiss, nothing like the ones they'd shared when they made love. But sensations ricocheted through him, nearly sending him to his knees.

He held it too long.

He kissed her too hard.

He just barely forced himself to pull back.

When he did, she finally looked at him. Her cheeks were flushed, her mouth bright red, and her silver-blue eyes were wide and vulnerable. Something smacked him square in the solar plexus, and he knew he was in very big trouble.

Even in the midst of her stressful wedding day, Stephanie's heart lifted when she saw McQuestin sitting on the front porch of the main ranch house. The old man was like a second grandfather to her, and she'd missed him while he'd been in Texas recovering from his broken leg.

She rushed out of Jared's SUV, leaving Alec in the backseat.

"You're home," she called, picking her way carefully along the pathway in her thin, impractical shoes.

The old man's smile was a slash across his weather-beaten face. His moustache and thick eyebrows were gray, and his hair, barely a fringe, was cut close to his head. His battered Stetson sat on his blue jean covered knee, while a pair of crutches were leaned against the wall next to his deck chair.

"Married?" he asked gruffly.

"I am," she admitted, giving him a hug and a kiss on his leathery cheek. She hoped her brothers hadn't told McQuestin about her pregnancy.

"How's the leg?" she asked, brushing past the subject of the wedding.

"Be right as rain in no time. This your gentleman?" He nodded past Stephanie.

Her hand still resting on McQuestin's shoulder, she turned to see Alec mount the stairs a few feet in front of Jared and Melissa. Royce's truck came to a halt behind the SUV.

"That's him," said Stephanie.

McQuestin looked Alec up and down. "She's too young to get married." An accusation and a challenge were both clear in his tone.

Alec stepped forward and wrapped an arm around Stephanie's bare shoulders. His hand was warm, strong and slightly callused, and her skin all but jumped under the touch.

"Sometimes a man has to move fast," he responded easily. "Couldn't take a chance on somebody else snapping her up."

McQuestin's faded blue eyes narrowed. "You're not stupid. I'll give you that."

"I told you you'd like him," Jared put in.

"Never said I liked him. Said he wasn't stupid. Now this one, I like." He nodded to Amber as she joined the group. "Got a good head on her shoulders."

"That she does," Royce agreed, and Stephanie realized McQuestin would only have met Amber today. Melissa on the other hand had been engaged to Jared before McQuestin's accident.

McQuestin glanced around at the circle of six. "You go away for a couple of months, and look what happens?"

The comparison of the three relationships made Stephanie uncomfortable. She shrugged out of Alec's embrace and backed toward the door. "I'll go see how Sasha's doing."

"She's got that table all decked out in delicates," said McQuestin. "I'm afraid to touch it."

"We're celebrating," said Melissa, giving him a hug on the way past. "It's good to have you back."

McQuestin winked at her. "A poker game with you later, young lady."

"You bet." Melissa fell into step behind Stephanie, passing through the doorway. "I think he lets me win," she confessed in a whisper.

"If you're winning, he's letting you," Stephanie confirmed.

"Who is he?" asked Amber as the door closed behind the three women. "We only had time for 'hi, how are you,' before we left for the ceremony."

"He's been the ranch manager forever," said Stephanie, slowing her steps as she approached the dining room table.

It was set with her mother's china, the best crystal wineglasses, an ornate, silver candelabra and low bouquets of wildflowers. Sheer curtains muted the lighting, and Sasha had baked a stunning, three tiered wedding cake. It was pure white, decorated with a cascade of mixed berries and was sitting on the sideboard with an ornate silver knife and a stack of china plates.

Stephanie gripped the back of a chair. "I feel like such a fraud."

"You're not a fraud," said Melissa, coming up on one side.

Amber came up on the other, flanking Stephanie with support. "And it looks delicious."

The unexpected observation made Stephanie smile. "Are we looking at the bright side?"

"No point in doing anything else."

"I suppose that's true," Stephanie allowed as she wandered over to the cake.

It did look delicious. She reached around the back, and swiped her fingertip through the icing then licked the sweetness off with her tongue.

"I can't believe you did that," Melissa laughed.

But Amber followed suit, tasting the icing herself. "Yum. Butter cream."

"It's good," Stephanie agreed.

"I love cake," Amber snickered.

Stephanie lifted the knife. "Let's cut it now."

"Oh, no, you don't." Melissa trapped her wrist.

Stephanie struggled to escape. "What? You worried it's bad luck."

"I don't believe in wedding luck," said Amber, swiping another finger full of icing. "My fiancé saw the wedding dress before the ceremony *and* slept with the bridesmaid. And that turned out to be good luck."

Stephanie and Melissa both blinked, round-eyed at Amber.

"Royce slept with a bridesmaid?" Stephanie asked in astonishment.

"Not Royce. My old fiancé, Hargrove. He slept with my best friend Katie. So I say to hell with luck. Let's eat the cake."

"Hello?" came Alec's censorious voice from the doorway.

Stephanie and Melissa both dropped the knife, and Amber guiltily jerked her finger away from the bottom layer.

"Amber has a thing for cake." Royce's tone was dry next to Alec, but there was a twinkle in his eyes exclusively for Amber.

"That's true," Amber admitted, grinning right back at him, making a show of licking the tip of her finger.

Something about their easy intimacy tightened Stephanie's chest. She didn't dare look at Alec, knowing his expression would be guarded. There was no intimacy between them. They were barely acquaintances.

A few words, no matter how official, couldn't make this a real marriage.

She knew she'd repeated the vows, and so had Alec, because the preacher had pronounced them husband and wife. But there'd been a ringing in her ears, and she'd had trouble focusing her eyes. She couldn't honestly say she recalled any of it.

Except the kiss. She remembered the kiss all too well. And she remembered her body's reaction to it—the arousal, the yearning, the fleeting fantasy that he'd scoop her into his arms and carry her off on a honeymoon.

"Stephanie?" Alec interrupted her thoughts.

Before she could stop herself, she glanced his way and caught his neutral expression, no twinkle, no teasing, no private message.

"The cake," he prompted. "It's up to the bride."

Amber playfully elbowed her in the ribs. "Let's do it."

Stephanie forced a carefree laugh, turning away from Alec. "I don't care if we cut it before dinner."

"Not without a picture," said Melissa.

Stephanie kept the smile determinedly pasted on her face. "Sure."

Alec dutifully moved up next to her and the ornate cake, draping an arm around Stephanie's shoulders.

Despite her vow to remain detached, she flinched under his touch.

"It'll all be over soon," he promised in a whisper.

"Maybe for you," she snapped. "You go right back to your regular life."

He stiffened. "You want me to stay?"

"Of course not." But she realized it was a lie.

She desperately wanted him to stay.

Six

It had been two weeks since Alec had seen or heard from Stephanie. Back in his compact, Chicago office, he'd filled every spare second with reviews of the various Ryder International divisions and queries to the possible whereabouts of Norman Stanton. He'd called in every outstanding favor and, quite literally, had feelers out all over the globe.

But no matter how hard he concentrated, he couldn't get Stephanie off his mind. He knew he had to stay well away from her for both their sakes, but he couldn't help wondering what she was doing. Was she still battling morning sickness? Was she picking out baby clothes? A crib? Thinking about a nursery? Had she been to the doctor again?

He was tempted to call, but he had to be strong. He'd seen the loneliness in her eyes and caught her fleeting glances his way after the wedding ceremony. She was vulnerable right now, and Alec couldn't risk having her look to him for emotional support.

His instinct to care for his wife and unborn child might be strong, but if he gave in, it would be Stephanie who got hurt in the end.

A news update droned in the corner on his small television set, while the cordless phone on his desktop sharply chimed.

It was an unfamiliar area code, and he snapped up the receiver. "Creighton here."

"Alec. It's Damien."

Anticipation tightened Alec's gut. "What've you got?"

"We found him."

Alec rocked forward in his chair, senses instantly alert. "Where?"

"Morocco."

Alec closed his eyes for a brief second of thankfulness. "Good. Great. What now?"

Damien Burke was a decorated, former military man. He'd done tours in both special forces and army intelligence, and there was nobody Alec trusted more.

"The U.S. doesn't have an extradition treaty with Morocco. Not that I'm suggesting we involve the Moroccan authorities. But Stanton will know that. You can bet that's why he's here. And that limits our bargaining power."

"It's not like we didn't expect this," said Alec. The man was smart enough to illegally drain millions of dollars from the Ryders then hide out in a foreign country. It stood to reason he'd done his research on extradition laws.

"I may be able to get him to Spain," Damien offered.

Alec was cautious. "How?" Kidnapping was not something he was prepared to authorize.

Damien chuckled, obviously guessing the direction of Alec's thoughts. "Margarita Castillo, Alec. Trust me, I'm not about to break the law and get myself thrown in a Moroccan jail."

"Who is she?"

"An associate who, I promise you, will have Norman Stanton on an airplane within twenty-four hours."

"And then?"

"And then a friend from Interpol will lay out the man's options."

Alec battled a moment's hesitation. "You won't do anything… You know…"

Damien scoffed. "'You know' won't be even remotely necessary. I've watched the man all day. He's soft as a tourist. We're shootin' fish in a barrel here."

"Good." A tentative satisfaction bloomed to life inside Alec. He might not be able to be with Stephanie in Montana, but he could do this for her.

Not that she'd ever find out.

"Touch base again tomorrow?" asked Damien.

"Thanks," said Alec, signing off and sliding the phone back into the charger.

"—arrived at Brighton earlier this morning," said the female, television news announcer, "and seen here heading for the barn area with her mare Rosie-Jo."

At the sound of the familiar name, Alec's gaze flicked to the television set.

"Anyone who follows the national circuit will remember this pair from Caldona where Stephanie Ryder and Rosie-Jo took first place."

Alec reflexively came to his feet, drinking in the sight of Stephanie's smiling face. She was dressed in faded jeans and a white cotton blouse. Her auburn hair was braided tight, and her amazing clear blue eyes sparkled in the Kentucky sunshine.

"She's had an extraordinary year," the male co-anchor put in.

"And an extraordinary career," said the female. "If they take the blue ribbon this weekend, you have to expect the pair to be a shoe-in for the Olympic team."

If they *what?*

"People are calling Rosie-Jo a cross between Big Ben and Miss Budweiser," the announcer continued.

Alec gave his head a startled shake.

This was Brighton.

It was live.

Stephanie wasn't allowed to jump. It was too dangerous for the baby.

"High praise, indeed," the other answered.

Alec knew she was unhappy about the pregnancy, and he knew how desperately she wanted to compete. But she wouldn't… She couldn't…

She stepped past a cluster of reporters, Wesley beside her, leading Rosie-Jo.

"What would it mean to you to win at Brighton?" one reporter asked her.

"I'm sorry?" she cocked her head to better hear above the noise.

"What makes Rosie-Jo so special?" asked another, drawing Stephanie's attention.

"Ambition." She smiled. "She's a powerful jumper, and she loves her job, so she's always totally enthusiastic. But she's still very careful."

Stephanie took a step back, giving a friendly wave but ignoring the rest of the questions.

Alec flipped open his cell phone, dialing hers as he

powered down his computer. He got her voice mail, left a
terse message to call him then tried Royce.

By the time Royce's voice mail kicked in, Alec was out
the door on his way to the airport. He didn't know what the
hell she was thinking. Forget about who was vulnerable
and who might get hurt, his job was to protect his unborn
child.

The reporter's question had startled Stephanie, so she'd
pretended not to hear it. Word that she'd scratched from the
competition had obviously not yet leaked out. But it would
be common knowledge by Friday at the latest, and there
would be questions, although she had no idea how she was
going to answer them.

Wesley turned Rosie-Jo into her appointed stall at the
Brighton grounds. His shoulders were tense, and he'd barely
said a word since they boarded the plane in Montana.

She'd been waiting since the wedding for his sullen
mood to lift. She kept thinking another day, another week,
and he'd stop acting like she'd kicked his dog.

He unclipped Rosie's lead rope, and the horse startled.

"Wesley," Stephanie sighed, knowing time was up. He
needed to focus completely on jumping, and that meant
she had to confront the situation head-on.

"Yeah?" He concentrated on coiling the lead rope in his
callused hands.

"You can't ride like this."

He didn't look up. "Ride like what?"

"You know what I'm talking about."

He crossed to the stall gate and slipped the catch. "I'm
fine."

"You're not fine."

He set his lips in a thin line, opening the gate.

She followed him out. "We need to talk—"

"It's none of your business."

"I'm your *coach*."

He glared at her, obviously struggling to mask the hurt with anger. "And I guess that's all you ever were."

Guilt tightened her chest. "Wesley, I never—"

"Never what? Never said we had a future? Never said you liked me? Never rushed off to marry that—"

"Wesley," she warned.

"Why did you lie?" The pain was naked in his eyes now. "All that stuff about us talking about it later. Why didn't you just tell me up-front it was him?"

Wesley was in worse shape than she'd realized, and she knew she had to talk him down. Riding Rosie-Jo at Brighton was a once in a lifetime chance for him to make a splash in front of a huge, national class audience.

"I didn't lie," she told him sincerely. "I do like you."

His lips thinned, and he turned to walk away.

She rushed after him, pushing her hesitation to a far corner of her mind. It was time to be completely honest. "I married Alec because I'm pregnant."

Wesley's head jerked back.

"We got married because of the baby."

He stopped and blinked at her in stunned silence.

"I don't know where it's going, or what will happen in the long-term. But I didn't lie to you, Wesley."

He glanced reflexively at her stomach. "That's why you're not riding."

"Yes."

"You mean…" His brain was obviously ticking through the math, going back to Alec's first visit to the ranch.

"Don't even go there," Stephanie warned, already

regretting her impulse. Her behavior was none of Wesley's business.

"Right." He squared his shoulders. "So it's a marriage of convenience. You're not in love with him."

She didn't answer.

After a beat of silence, the pain and anger cleared from Wesley's eyes. Then he smiled. "So, afterward…"

In an instant, Stephanie realized her error. His hopes were up all over again.

It took Alec the rest of the afternoon to get from Chicago to Lexington and take the short hop to Cedarvale and the Brighton facility.

He tried Stephanie's cell phone again, then tracked down her hotel and had the front desk try her room. In the end, he was forced to talk his way into the restricted area of the grounds and walk methodically through the horse barns looking for her.

He finally spotted her in the distance, outside, next to a white rail fence line decorated with sponsor bulletin boards.

Even at this distance, she took his breath away. The late day sunshine glinted off her hair. She was silhouetted against a dark background, her jeans and white blouse accentuating the body that he adored. He swore he could hear her voice, her laughter, her gasps when he drew her against him and kissed her.

It was all in his mind, of course. He was deluding himself if he thought she'd ever laugh with him again after this.

He wished he didn't have to be mad at her. He didn't want to fight. He wanted to hold her in his arms, caress her and kiss her, tell her everything was going to be okay. Then he wanted to figure out a way to make it okay.

For a moment he wondered if he'd played it wrong at their wedding. She'd asked him to leave, but if he'd stuck around, maybe she wouldn't be here. Their baby would be safe. And he wouldn't be headed for a confrontation that was sure to hurt them both.

As he drew closer still, he saw she was talking to a couple of reporters. Despite his simmering anger, he had to give her kudos for that.

But then he saw who was standing beside her. Wesley again. And the kid was way too close. They were practically touching. While Alec marched forward, Wesley reached up and cupped his hand over her shoulder, giving it a squeeze.

Alec quickened his pace.

The sun was setting, but the barn area was still alive with activity. Grooms walked horses, stable hands moved feed and manure, while technicians worked in the broadcast tents, setting up sound and video equipment for the weekend.

Alec halted beside Stephanie, and in one swift motion wrapped his arm around her shoulder, dislodging Wesley's hand.

Stephanie turned to stare at him. While Wesley's head whipped around. Both reporters immediately stopped talking. And the television camera swung to Alec.

"Alec Creighton," he introduced himself with a nod. "Stephanie's husband."

Stephanie froze beneath his embrace, while the two female reporters' jaws dropped open.

"Sorry to interrupt, darling," he put in easily.

One reporter recovered more quickly and stuffed her microphone in Alec's face. "You're married to Stephanie Ryder."

"Stephanie Creighton," Alec corrected, though they'd never actually discussed her changing her name.

"When did you get married?"

"Tell us about the wedding."

"We were married in Montana. At the Ryder Ranch." Alec made a show of smiling down at Stephanie. "It was a simple ceremony, just the family."

The reporters switched their attention to Stephanie.

"This is big news. Were you planning a formal announcement?"

Alec didn't give Stephanie a chance to speak. Not that she seemed particularly capable of joining the conversation.

"You can take this as a formal announcement," he told them. "You can also take this as notification that Stephanie won't be competing this weekend."

Both microphones went to Stephanie. "You're not competing?"

"Thank you," said Alec. "That's all we have to say for the moment." He swiftly turned her away and started back across the yard.

"You *did not* just do that," Stephanie rasped as they angled across the lawn to the nearest building.

Wesley seemed to have found his feet and was struggling to catch up with them.

"What are you doing here?" Alec demanded of Stephanie.

"What do you mean?"

Wesley caught them at a trot, and Alec pasted him with a warning glare.

Was the kid suicidal?

Stephanie was Alec's wife. Wesley had absolutely no right to be touching her.

"This is a private conversation," Alec announced.

Wesley looked to Stephanie for confirmation, and it was all Alec could do not to send the man sprawling.

"It's okay, Wesley," said Stephanie. "I don't know what he's doing here, but—"

"Goodbye, Wesley," Alec interrupted.

Wesley hesitated a second longer in a transparent and hopeless attempt to pretend he had a choice. Then he shot Alec a hostile look and peeled off to one side, tracking for one of the technical tents.

Stephanie stopped dead. "What is the *matter* with you?"

"Not here," Alec growled, scanning the grounds, looking for a place that offered privacy. It didn't seem promising.

"We'll go back to the hotel." He switched their direction.

"Those were reporters," she hissed under her breath.

"No kidding."

"An hour from now, everybody's going to know we're married."

"Were you planning to keep it a secret?"

"No. I don't know. I hadn't really thought about it."

"What about the baby? Were you planning to keep that a secret, too?"

"Yes. For now anyway."

He grunted, struggling to hold his temper.

She didn't seem to feel guilty. She didn't seem contrite. Had she somehow convinced herself it was okay to fly eight feet in the air and come crashing down on the back of a eighteen-hundred-pound animal? He'd seen her last bruise. The sport was bloody dangerous.

They took a stone pathway to the main hotel tower, crossed the lobby and entered an elevator.

As the elevator filled up, Alec nabbed her hand and

tugged her close beside him. She pressed the button for the twenty-sixth floor.

It was a short walk down the hallway to her room. She inserted the key. He opened the door. Then he shut it behind them.

She immediately turned on him, back to the picture window that looked over the arena. "Are you out of your mind?"

He ignored the question. "Do your brothers know you're here?"

"Of course they know I'm here. Why are you acting like I've done something wrong?"

He advanced on her. "Because you're *pregnant*."

"I know I'm pregnant. That doesn't mean my life stops."

"*This* part of your life stops."

She paused. Her eyes darkened. Then she waggled her finger at him, stepping three paces backward as she shook her head. "Oh, no, no, no. I am not going to sit home in Montana twiddling my thumbs for the next seven months."

He stepped forward once again. "Well you're sure as *hell* not sitting on the back of a horse jumping six-foot oxers."

She blinked. "What?"

"I know you can be reckless. I've heard you're irresponsible. But honest-to-God, Stephanie—"

"*What?*" she shouted.

"You are *not* going to compete in show jumping while you're pregnant with my baby."

She stared at him like he'd grown two heads. "What makes you think I'm competing?"

He gestured out the picture window. "You're here."

"I'm coaching Wesley."

Nice try. "With Rosie-Jo?"

"Wesley's riding her."

"No, he's not." The woman was caught. She might as well own up to it.

"Yes, he is."

"Rosie-Jo is your horse."

"She's also a once-in-a-lifetime jumper. She's not taking a year off just because I'm forced to."

Alec stopped. A chill of unease spread through him. "You're not jumping?"

"Of course I'm not jumping, you idiot. It's dangerous."

"I *know*. That's why I'm here."

Her shoulders relaxed. "To stop me from jumping?"

"Yes."

"I don't understand, Alec." She gave her head a little shake. "Where did you get the idea...?"

He raked a hand through his hair. "I saw you on television this afternoon. You were here. You had Rosie-Jo. The reporters—"

"And you jumped to a conclusion."

"Apparently."

Her eyes narrowed. "Where were you?"

"Chicago."

"And you flew all the way to Cedarvale?"

"What was I supposed to do?"

"Phone me?"

"I tried."

"Trust me?"

Alec didn't have an answer for that. How could he trust her? He barely knew her.

"It's my baby, too, Alec."

"I know."

"I'm not going to hurt our baby."

Alec drew a breath. He supposed he knew that now. But he had no way of knowing that back in Chicago when the evidence had stacked up against her.

The hotel room telephone jangled.

Stephanie kept him in her sights with a censorious expression as she crossed to answer it.

"Hello?"

She paused. "Yes."

She nodded. "Okay… I know… Thank you."

She hung up the phone then turned to Alec.

"What is it?"

"Word's getting around. You've just been included on a VIP reception invitation for tomorrow night."

She waited, and Alec wasn't sure what to say.

"What are you going to do?" she finally asked.

He knew what he should say, knew he should get his butt back on that plane and leave her the heck alone. But now that he was here, he couldn't bring himself to leave. He found his emotions making deals with his conscience.

He promised himself it would only be for a day or two. He'd get them a suite, so they both had privacy. He wouldn't let her get close, wouldn't let her depend on him. He wouldn't do anything to mislead her.

But when he spoke, his voice came out soft and deliberate. "I guess I'll stick around and be your husband."

"This way," Stephanie said to Alec, pointing to an aisle that stretched between two racks of clothes in the exhibition hall in the basement of the hotel. For the first time in weeks, she felt lighter, almost happy. She'd always enjoyed the social events around major jumping competitions, and she woke up this morning vowing to enjoy them this weekend.

It would be odd hanging out with Alec, odder still that people would know they were married. But at least she'd have a dancing partner.

She supposed there was always a silver lining.

"You have got to be kidding me." Alec stopped dead in his tracks in the middle of the exhibition hall entrance, staring in obvious disbelief at the racks of costumes, hats, shoes and accessories.

"Our party's a 1920s theme," she offered, halting beside him.

He gazed deliberately around the barnlike costume rental setup. "They bring all this in for horse jumping?"

"Tonight isn't the only theme event. And with this many wealthy people in one place, it's a prime opportunity for fund-raising."

People were starting to pile up behind them, so she snagged his arm and tugged him forward.

"You mean I have to dress up in a costume *and* give away my money?" he asked.

"You really don't get out much, do you?" she couldn't help teasing him.

"Not like this," he told her, gazing around the jumble of merchandise taking up about a quarter of the cavernous room. "I'm more a dinner at Palazzo Antinori or a cruise on the Seine kind of guy."

"A closet romantic," she reflexively observed, then cringed at the unfortunate choice of words.

His expression turned serious. "No, Stephanie. I'm not a romantic of any kind."

She sensed some kind of a warning in his words.

"Over there." She cheerfully pointed, changing the subject as they made their way past a suit of medieval armor and a shelf of colored wigs and sparkling Mardi Gras masks.

Alec leaned in close, his tone still dire. "I don't want you to…" He obviously struggled for words.

She refused to prompt him. She really didn't want to pursue this line of conversation.

"To get caught up—"

"In the 1920s?" she wedged in.

"In our marriage," he corrected.

She let sarcasm color her tone. "You afraid I'll mistake a dance for a declaration of undying passion and devotion?"

He backed off a little. "You seem…"

"What?" she demanded.

He shrugged. "Happy. Animated."

"And you attribute that to *you?* Wow. That's some ego you've got going there Alec."

"It's not my ego."

"Right."

He clenched his jaw. "Forget I said anything."

"I will."

"Good."

"You're faking, Alec. I get that. I'm faking it, too." She might have let her emotional guard down for a moment, but she wouldn't make the mistake of enjoying herself again.

He searched her expression. "Fine."

"Fine." She nodded in return. Just flipping fine. Bad enough she had to fake a marriage. Now she wasn't allowed to smile while she did it.

She put her attention on the costume racks again, now simply wanting to get this over with. "You might as well pick something?"

He glanced around. "I'm not a fan of costumes."

"Yeah? Too bad."

He shot her a look of annoyance.

What? She was supposed to get happy again? "Be a man about it," she challenged. "Put on some pinstripes and spats. Be grateful it's not superhero night."

His look of horror almost made her smile.

"You'd look good in red tights."

"Not in this lifetime."

"Check those out." She gestured to a rack of suit jackets.

For herself, she moved further down the aisle, finding a selection of flapper dresses.

She started through them one by one. After a few minutes, she came across a sexy, silky black sheath, dripping with shimmering silver ribbons that flowed from the low-cut neckline, past the short hem of the underdress to knee-length.

With a spurt of mischievousness, she held it against her body. "What do you think?"

His gaze traveled the length of the garment, eyes glittering with what looked suspiciously like humor. "You show up in that, doll-face, and I'd better be packin' heat."

This time, she did crack a smile.

She pulled the dress away from her body, turning it and making a show of taking a critical look. "Too much?"

"Not nearly enough."

She could have sworn there was a sensual edge to his tone. But his cell phone chimed, cutting it off.

She hung the dress back on the rack, battling a wave of prickly heat that slowly throbbed its way through her system. Faking, she reminded herself ruthlessly. Faking, faking, faking.

"Alec Creighton," he said into the phone.

His glance darted to her for a split second, then he turned away, lowering his voice.

She told herself to focus on the costumes and give him his privacy. He had his own life, and she had hers. As he'd so clearly just pointed out, this intersection between them was completely temporary.

Still, she couldn't help catching snatches of the conversation. She heard him say tomorrow, then airport, then Cedarvale.

It sounded like he was leaving, and a wave of disappointment surprised and worried her. It was good that he was leaving.

But then she heard him say her brothers' names. She blinked at his back, listening unabashedly to the final snatches of the conversation.

As he signed off, she quickly grabbed another dress, pretending to be absorbed by it.

"This one?" she asked.

It was a soft, champagne silk, with a low V-neck, spaghetti straps and covered in sparkling, criss-cross beading. The silk came to midthigh, while a wide, sheer, metallic lace hemline, slashed to points, rustled around her knees.

"They don't have anything with sleeves?" he frowned.

"It's the roaring twenties," she told him, trying not to wonder about his phone call. "I'm supposed to look like your moll. What do you think? A wide choker and a long string of pearls?"

"I think you'll be the death of me."

"What about the red one?" she lifted another from the rack. "It comes with satin gloves and a feather boa.

Alec's nostrils flared. "Better stick with the gold."

"It's champagne."

"Not the red, and definitely not the black."

"Fine." She put the red one back, wishing she was brave enough to ask about the phone call. Was he leaving? And why had he mentioned her brothers? "What about a long cigarette holder?" she asked instead.

"Absolutely not. You're pregnant."

"Shhhh." She glanced quickly around, worried someone would overhear.

He moved closer, leaning down to whisper. "You're pregnant."

"I wouldn't really smoke anything."

"Don't even joke about it."

"Who was on the phone?" she blurted out.

"A friend."

"Does he know my brothers?"

Alec's brow furrowed. "No. Why?"

"No reason," she lied, glancing away. "I thought it might be about the Ryder International review. Are you leaving tomorrow?"

"You trying to get rid of me?"

She looked back up at him again, puzzling over why he'd hold back the truth about the phone call. If the friend didn't know her brothers, Alec wouldn't have mentioned their names. "I need to get Wesley prepared," she told him.

Alec's jaw tightened, eyes squinting further. "I'm staying."

"Okay," she agreed.

He gave a sharp nod of acknowledgment.

Moving away from yet another uncomfortable moment, she gestured to the rack of suits. "Did you find something to wear?"

"I'm not wearing pinstripes."

"How about a hat?" She selected one with a center dent and a wide, satin band and tried to place it on his head.

He jerked sideways, out of the way. "How about a suit jacket and a pair of slacks, and I write a check big enough that nobody cares?"

Seven

Chandeliers dangled from the ballroom ceiling, while massive ice sculptures and floral arrangements decorated white linen tables. The waiters wore period tuxedoes, and a big band played a jazz tune on a low stage in one corner of the room.

On Alec's arm, Stephanie glittered. Her rich, auburn hair bounced in a halo of tight curls to her bare shoulders. It was pulled back on one side by an elaborate, rhinestone clip, which matched her ornate necklace and dangling earrings. Her makeup had been done in a bright twenties-style, and the shimmering, champagne dress clung to her lithe body.

Alec couldn't help a surge of pride as people turned to stare. His marriage might be a sham, but he was the envy of every man in the room.

He leaned down to whisper. "You should dress up like a girl more often."

"They're not looking at me," she whispered back, smiling politely at the onlookers.

"Yes, they are." More people turned to stare.

Up to now, it hadn't occurred to Alec to wonder how Stephanie had made it to twenty-two as a virgin. But now it sure did. He also realized men would be lining up to take his place the minute he was out of the picture.

It was not a pleasant thought.

"They've heard," she told him in an undertone.

"Heard what?"

"About us. That we got married."

He disagreed. "It's you." Still, at the mention of his temporary position, he couldn't stop himself from curling his arm around the small of her back.

"Oh, sure," she mocked. "Really give them something to talk about."

"I could give you a kiss."

"You're incorrigible."

"Just playing my part."

"Play it from over there." She quickly sidestepped out of his embrace.

He followed, snagging her around the waist once more. "And how will that be convincing?"

"Give it your best effort."

"Oh, I intend to," he drawled.

"Stephanie," purred a woman in a floor-length, peacock-blue, sequined gown. She swept in front of them with a flourish, looking to be about sixty-five, though very well preserved. Her streaked blond hair was decorated with blue feathers, and she brandished a matching fan like a weapon.

"Mrs. Cleary," Stephanie greeted with a smile, and the woman's gaze immediately jumped to Alec. She raised her sculpted brows.

"This is my husband, Alec Creighton," Stephanie supplied smoothly.

Alec liked the sound of that. He let his hand slip to hers, and he stroked the pad of his thumb across her diamond ring and the matching wedding band.

Stephanie jolted her hand away. "Mrs. Cleary is the president of the Brighton Fund-raising Committee." The tone told him he ought to be impressed.

"A pleasure, Mrs. Cleary." He gave her a warm smile and used his newly freed hand to shake with her.

She checked him over carefully. "Please, call me Bridget."

"Bridget," he obliged.

"I hear congratulations are in order." The words were more an accusation than a tribute.

"Indeed, they are." Alec drew Stephanie firmly to his side, feeling her soft curves beneath the sexy dress. There was no law telling him he couldn't enjoy his acting role. "We're looking forward to starting a family."

He felt her stiffen, but how could she complain? He was simply smoothing the pathway for the inevitable announcement of her pregnancy.

"Stephanie?" came a second voice, a younger woman this time. "Are you going to introduce me?" She offered Alec a gleaming white, perfectly straight orthodontic smile.

She looked to be in her late twenties and wore a bright purple, beaded dress, and a matching headband. She held a long cigarette holder, and her blond hair was upswept in a riot of curls. Her lashes were dark with heavy makeup, and she wore fishnet stockings with high-heeled, black shoes accented by an oversize silver buckle on the sexy ankle strap.

In another time and another place, he would have smiled right back at the undeniably beautiful woman. She was the stuff of erotic dreams. But Alec found he preferred Stephanie's more understated look. And it wasn't just the fake husband in him speaking. Interesting.

"Rene," Stephanie greeted, her voice slightly tight, features carefully neutral. "This is my husband, Alec."

There was a proprietary inflection on the word husband. Nice.

"Pleasure to meet you, Alec the husband," Rene giggled as she extended the back of her hand, wiggling her fingers in an obvious invitation.

He ignored the hint, and shook her hand instead of kissing the back.

She gave a mock pout with her jewel-red lips.

A tall, thin man appeared. He wore an outrageous purple velvet coat with leopard-print trim and matching slacks.

"Rene," he admonished, from beneath a broad brimmed hat. Then he glared a warning at Alec.

Alec had to bite down hard to keep from laughing. It was tough to take a man seriously when he was dressed like a sitcom pimp.

"Alec Creighton," he said instead and extended his hand. "I believe our wives know each other."

The man's eyes went round.

"Wife?" Rene cackled. "That'll be the day."

"My apologies," said Alec. Then he smiled warmly down at Stephanie. "But I highly recommend it." He glanced back at the man. "You should think about asking her."

The man looked like a deer in the headlights.

Alec could feel Stephanie's body vibrate with repressed laughter.

"What do you think, sweetheart?" Alec asked her.

"Dance," she sputtered, grabbing Alec's arm and turning him away from Rene.

Alec quickly took the lead as they wove their way through the crowd.

"You are *bad*," Stephanie accused.

"They deserved it. So, who is she?"

"She's the princess of the circuit. Her father owns a stable of jumping horses."

"Big deal. So do you."

Stephanie snorted out a laugh. "Not like he does."

Alec drew her into his arms and swung her into the latest song in a Duke Ellington tribute. "You're not intimidated are you?"

"By Rene?" Stephanie easily followed his lead.

"Yes." He waited. He'd learned to recognize it when she was stalling.

She paused. "Maybe once. She's been glamorous since she was twelve."

"You're glamorous now."

Stephanie coughed out a laugh. "Not like her."

Alec let his hand trail along the smooth silk of Stephanie's dress, letting the tactile memory remind him of exactly how gorgeous she'd looked walking out of her hotel bedroom earlier. She'd positively taken his breath away.

Now, his voice went husky. "Better than her."

She didn't answer, but she seemed to mold slightly closer against him. He gathered her tight, ignoring the warning that was sounding in his brain.

"Besides," he forced himself to joke. "She's obviously jealous of your husband."

"Ego, Alec?"

"A man can tell these things."

"Because she was flirting with you?"

"Exactly."

Stephanie chuckled. "She flirts with everyone."

"I'm quite a catch," he protested, telling himself to put a little distance between their bodies.

He ignored himself.

"You have quite the ego."

"Part of my charm."

"You have charm?"

He didn't answer. Instead he savored the feel of her in his arms, inhaling the scent of her hair, letting the haunting strains of a saxophone solo carry them away.

"I suppose you do," she said softly.

"What?"

"Have charm."

He drew back. "You're conceding a point?"

"You also have looks," she continued. "But you already know that. Every woman in the room is envious of me right now."

"You mean every man is envious of me." He drew a breath. "How is it," he struggled to frame the question that had been nagging at him for weeks. "That you stayed a virgin all those years?"

"I don't get out much."

"I'm serious."

"So am I."

"Stephanie?"

She shrugged against him. "I honestly never had any offers."

Now that was ridiculous. He chuckled low. "Maybe there weren't any verbal offers. But, trust me, there were offers. You've had at least two dozen since you walked into this room."

She pulled back. "Where?"

"Never mind."

"You're crazy."

"I'm just smarter than you."

She rolled her eyes.

"More observant," he amended.

"You have a vivid imagination."

"And you have a sexy rear end."

"You keep your mind off my— *Hey,* there's Royce. What's he doing here?"

Alec didn't know whether to resent the interruption or be grateful Royce had arrived so promptly.

Before he could make up his mind, Stephanie was out of his arms and heading off the dance floor.

Alec followed closely behind.

She glanced from her brother to Amber. "Where did you guys come from?"

Amber grinned, but her quick glance at Alec told him she knew they were here about Stanton.

"We were in Chicago," she told Stephanie. "But you know your brother. I mentioned you might need moral support, and the next thing I knew we were taxiing down the tarmac."

Stephanie's brows knit together. "But I'm not even riding."

"Exactly," said Amber, drawing Stephanie a small distance away from Alec and Royce.

Royce gave him a nod. "I got your voice mail."

"Damien has news," Alec returned. "Amber knows?"

Royce stepped closer and kept his voice low. "Amber's the brains of the outfit. She was the one that noticed the resemblance between Frank's sister and Stephanie."

Alec nodded. "You have an intelligent fiancée."

"I have an amazing fiancée."

Alec's gaze strayed to Amber's black and red costume. The women were drawing more than their share of appreciative male glances. "You might want to hurry up and marry her."

Royce looked around, clearly making the same observation as Alec. "She's having trouble deciding on the wedding location." His shoulders squared. "But we might have to make a detour through Nevada on the way home."

Alec gave a chopped chuckle, while Royce took a half step toward Stephanie and Amber to stare a man down.

The man moved on, and Royce drew back. "What time's the meeting?"

"Wesley has a warm-up scheduled at three. Stephanie has to be there. I told Damien I'd call when the coast was clear."

"He's here?"

"On his way." It would be good news. Alec might not have heard the details yet, but if Damien was finished in Spain, Norman Stanton was no longer going to be a threat to the Ryders.

"How do we know Stanton won't go back on his word?" Royce asked Damien.

Alec had waited until Stephanie was occupied in the arena with Wesley and Rosie-Jo, then he'd given the all clear signal to Damien, Jared, Royce, Melissa and Amber. The group had assembled in the hotel suite's living room.

Jared nodded to back up his brother's question. "The man's a blackmailer and a thief."

Damien cast a fleeting glance to Alec. He wasn't used to having his situational assessment questioned. But he was also a consummate professional, so he wouldn't make an issue.

"Norman knows we can reach out and touch him in Morocco," he answered simply.

Alec straightened from where he'd propped his shoulder against the arched entryway to the dining area. "There aren't a lot of places left for him to hide."

"He must be pretty ticked off," Melissa put in. "What's to stop him from calling a tabloid and exposing it to the world?"

"Arrest and incarceration," said Alec.

Jared elaborated. "Stanton must have thought he was safe in Morocco. Yet Damien tracked him down and lured him to Spain. He knows we're tenacious, and he has to be feeling like there aren't a lot of places left to hide."

"Could the police really extradite him from Spain?" asked Royce.

Damien gave a little half smile. "Technically, yes. Practically… It's hard to say. But if you're Norman Stanton, do you take that chance?"

"We've got him trapped in a standoff," Alec clarified. "He talks to Stephanie, we press charges."

"A smart man takes the money and runs." Jared nodded.

"Any chance we can get the money back?" asked Amber. Then she glanced around at the blank faces. "We're talking about twelve million dollars here."

"I can look into it," said Damien. "But he'll have spent a lot of it already."

Royce shook his head. "I'm done. Stephanie's the important thing. I say if he walks away, we walk away."

Melissa's eyes went wide. "Excuse me? Twelve million dollars?" She glanced to Jared, and it was obvious the sum was news to her.

"Paid out over at least ten years," Jared told his wife.

"It was Grandpa Benteen and McQuestin," Amber elaborated. "They didn't know how else to—" She stopped, suddenly casting a guilty glance to Jared, obviously realizing Melissa might not know about Stephanie's illegitimacy.

"We have another problem," Alec told the gathering.

Everyone went silent.

He snagged one of the dining room chairs, straddling it backward in the archway and propping his elbows on the back.

Damien backed off a few steps, positioning himself near the glass patio door.

"Your mother was six months older than your father," Alec explained to Jared and Royce, trying to keep it as straightforward as possible. "Since they died together, she was deemed to have predeceased him."

Both men watched him, expressions growing wary.

"In his will, should his wife predecease him, your father asked that his estate 'be divided among my children, then alive.'"

There was a split second before the words sank in.

"Stephanie's not his child," said Jared.

"Frank Stanton." Melissa shook her head.

"But we can fix it?" Royce asked.

"I talked to Katie Merrick. It'll take a few lawyers, and a stack of contracts, but it's doable. Trick is, you'll have to get Stephanie to sign them without reading them."

"Too late for that." Stephanie's terse voice intruded.

Alec jerked his head toward her.

Stephanie stood in the foyer doorway. Her face was pale, but her eyes glittered with anger.

"Oh, no," Amber rasped.

Alec came to his feet.

Stephanie stared at her bothers. "I'm…" That was as far as she made it.

Both of them stood, but she held up a hand to stop them. "And nobody was going to *tell* me?" She turned her accusing stare on Alec.

"What did you hear?" he asked, his mind scrambling for a damage control plan.

"Is this a conspiracy?" She glanced around the room. Her gaze stopped on Damien. "Who's this?"

Damien glanced to Alec.

"He's yours," Stephanie scoffed at Alec. "Of course he's yours. Is this why they hired you?"

Alec took a step forward. "Stephanie."

"Wow." She gave a shaky laugh. "Is that what you're doing for us? Is Ryder International even *in* financial trouble?"

"Stephanie," Jared began.

"You should sit down," Royce put in.

Stephanie rounded on him. "*You* should start talking."

The two stared at each other for a moment.

"We were being blackmailed," said Royce.

"By Alec?"

"*No,*" Alec jumped in, unable to remain silent any longer. "By Norman Stanton. I *was* looking into your finances." He wasn't about to hit Royce and Jared with an *I told you so,* but it was darn tempting.

"So you claim." Stephanie glared at him. "But we both know you can fake pretty much anything."

"Alec's not the bad guy," said Amber.

"Then who's the bad guy?"

"Frank Stanton," said Royce.

"And he's my father?"

"Can we talk about this later?" asked Royce, his gaze going pointedly to Damien.

"Sure." Stephanie shrugged. "Don't mind me." She crossed to a desk and picked up some papers. "I just dropped by for the insurance forms. Let me know how this all turns out. I'll sign anything you want."

"Don't start sulking," warned Jared.

Alec felt a flash of anger. He moved to position himself between the two. "I think she's got a right to be a little upset," he told Jared.

Jared's eyes narrowed down. "Stay out of it."

"I don't believe I will." Alec folded his arms across his chest. They were the ones that hired him. They insisted he marry Stephanie. Convenience or not, she was his wife.

Royce stepped up beside his brother. "It's a family matter."

"I'm family."

"Not really."

"I have a piece of paper that says so."

Stephanie stepped back in. "And they have a piece of paper that says *I'm* not. Procured by *you*, if I overheard correctly."

"You're still our sister," Jared hastily put in.

"Half sister. Out of the will."

"There you go again," Royce all but shouted. "The most dramatic possible—"

"I think you'd better leave," Alec said to the brothers.

"Us leave?" Jared's voice was incredulous. "*You* leave."

"It's my hotel room. And she's my wife—"

"Give me a break!" Stephanie threw up her hands. "*I'll* leave."

"No." Alec's hand shot out to stop her. "We need to talk." Past today, they were still having a baby, and they still had to make that work.

"Let go of Stephanie," Royce growled.

Amber came to her feet, voice commanding. "Stop this. All of you. I mean it."

She placed herself between Alec and Royce. "Alec wants to talk to Stephanie."

Royce clamped his jaw in silent protest, but everyone filed out. Alec was left alone with Stephanie. "For the record," he told her, "I advised them to tell you the truth."

She didn't turn around. "Why didn't you tell me the truth?"

"I promised I wouldn't."

She was silent for a moment. "So a business contract is more important to you than your wedding vows?"

Alec drew a breath.

"Never mind," she continued. "Don't answer that."

He moved a few steps toward her. "It was complicated. I had no right—"

She turned. "No right to be honest with your wife?"

"Don't twist things to score points."

The woman had enough on her side of this argument without doing that.

She dropped into one of the French provincial chairs. "So, I guess I'm a bastard."

He pulled out another chair and angled it toward hers, sitting down. "So am I. It's not so bad."

"I meant literally, not metaphorically."

"So did I."

Her expression softened ever so slightly. "Really?"

"My father eventually married my mother." Though that had turned out to be more a curse than a blessing.

Stephanie slumped back in the chair. "My mother had an affair."

"So it would seem."

"I've had her up on a pretty high pedestal all these years."

Alec leaned forward, covering Stephanie's hands where they rested in her lap. "She was human."

"You accept infidelity?"

"I understand weakness and imperfection."

"Are you imperfect, Alec?"

"I took your virginity and made you pregnant while I was working for your brothers. Then I lied to you. Well, held back the truth anyway."

"And you'll eventually be unfaithful."

He drew back. "What? No. Why would I—"

"Can you really stay celibate for months on end?"

"I don't know," he admitted. He'd never tried.

It had only been a couple of weeks since the wedding, but so far he hadn't had any overwhelming desire to sleep with other women. Ironically the only person he wanted to make love to was Stephanie.

"You'll eventually give into temptation," she determined.

"Where is this coming from?"

"My mother did. Your parents did. We did."

"You've really wandered off on a tangent here." He wanted to talk about her family, to make sure she was coping okay with the truth.

"I'm merely pointing out that we both have the infidelity gene."

He coughed out a surprised laugh. "It comes down to principles and personal choice."

"*We* slept together."

The reminder made him aware of their joined hands, her sweet scent and those cherry-red lips that were slightly parted with her breath.

"Yes, we did," he agreed.

"When we shouldn't have."

"That's debatable. We didn't betray anyone."

"Except maybe ourselves."

Alec shifted his chair closer and raised their joined hands. "Do you feel guilty, Stephanie?"

She gazed into his eyes. "Do you?"

He shook his head. "I don't have a single regret about making love to you. And I don't hate Frank Stanton. And I'm glad your mother gave into temptation. If not for that, you wouldn't be here."

"So, I should be grateful?"

"You should be sensible. Don't rail against things you can't change. Just make the best of what you have."

She seemed to think about that for a minute. Then her lips softened, and her voice went low. "I miss you, Alec."

Desire instantly overran his brain. "I'm right here."

"That's not what I meant."

"I know." He steeled himself against the urge to drag her into his arms. "But you're upset and vulnerable, and I still have a few principles left."

Silver sparkled to life deep in her eyes. "How can I get rid of them?"

Simply by breathing. His hands convulsed around hers. "You can't."

A sharp rap sounded on the suite door, and Stephanie frowned.

Alec felt like he'd been saved from himself. They were only going to stay away so long.

Eight

"You know Stephanie's going to see him," Amber warned Royce in an undertone.

Alec slowed his steps, not wanting to intrude on what was obviously a private conversation, but wanting to know about anything that involved Stephanie.

She and her brothers had talked late into the night. Then Alec had seen her briefly at breakfast. But Wesley was in final preparation for competing tomorrow, so Stephanie's entire day was being spent at the arena. It annoyed Alec that Wesley was still flirting with her.

Royce gave Alec a nod of welcome. "I'm half tempted to buy it for her," Royce said to Amber.

"You know you can't do that," Amber returned. "The price tag's up over a million dollars."

"Hey, Alec," Royce greeted, and Amber turned around to face him.

Alec wished he could ask what they were debating. He hoped there weren't any more family secrets being kept from Stephanie.

He settled for, "What's up?"

"Blanchard's Run is here," said Amber.

Alec nodded, hoping to bluff his way through the conversation.

"Stephanie's still upset," said Royce.

"You can't buy her a million dollar horse to make her feel better," warned Amber, jabbing Royce with her elbow. "Tell him, Alec."

"She's right," Alec agreed. Stephanie didn't need monetary bribes from her brothers. She needed them to respect her enough to be honest with her.

"She's had her eye on him for months," said Royce.

"Here she is now," Alec warned them, as Stephanie approached from the opposite end of the barn. Her smooth, sexy stride carried swiftly along in her tooled cowboy boots.

Amber and Royce both turned.

"Uh-oh," Amber breathed.

Stephanie's attention had been caught by one of the stalls. She stopped and drew back in obvious surprise. Then she turned to walk to the gate.

She stood there for a few moments staring at the horse inside. Then she squared her shoulders and resumed walking toward them.

Nobody said a word as she approached.

"You knew, didn't you?" she asked her brother.

"We just found out," Amber quickly put in.

Stephanie cocked her head as she gazed steadily at Royce.

"We just saw him," he backed Amber up.

"But you weren't going to tell me."

They didn't deny it.

"Was that for my own good, too?"

When nobody immediately answered, she shook her head in disgust then paced off down the center aisle of the barn toward the hotel and the main offices.

Alec went quickly after her. "What was that about?"

She didn't break her stride. "Blanchard's Run."

"He's a horse, right?"

"He is."

"And you want to buy him?"

"I do."

"But he's expensive." Alec had the full picture now.

"He's a bargain."

"A million dollars?"

"You're just like the rest of them."

"Hold up there for a second." He snagged her arm, tugged her to a stop before she could exit the barn and join the crowds outside.

She stopped, but turned on him, eyes blazing.

"Is this important?" he asked.

"Not at all," she denied.

"Stephanie?"

She drew in an impatient sigh and crossed her arms beneath her breasts. "Why do you want to know?"

"Because I do. Because you're not mad at me, you're mad at them." He jabbed his thumb back in Royce's direction. "And because I hate it when you act like a spoiled kid."

Her eyes narrowed.

"You're not, you know. You're an intelligent woman who knows what she wants and how to work for it. You want this horse, and I'm curious to know why."

"Fine." She drew a breath. "I've been interested in

Blanchard's Run for nearly a year. I've studied his blood-lines and the conformation of his offspring, along with their competition records. And I think the combination of Blanchard's Run and my retired mare, Pinnacle, would produce fast, smart, high jumpers. If science and genetics has anything to say about it, the EBVs of their offspring would be off the charts."

"EBVs?"

"Estimated Breeding Value."

"Oh."

"In technical terms, they would be worth a whole lot of money."

"Really?"

"Yes, really. I can also breed him to three other mares I've bought this year, partly in anticipation of a future acquisition of Blanchard's Run. Then, three, maybe five years from now, if his existing offspring prove out the way I expect them to, and if the Ryder foals show promise, we'll be able to get top dollar for the animals."

Alec was impressed. "So, why don't your brothers want you to buy the horse?"

"Because they've never listened long enough to know my plan is based on concrete science. They assume I'm operating on emotion instead of intelligence."

"They're wrong," said Alec.

"Yeah? Well, since I'm out of the will, I don't have much of a leg to stand on anymore."

"There is that." Even as Alec was agreeing with her, he was coming to a decision.

It had nothing to do with guilt. And it had nothing to do with his feelings for Stephanie. And it wasn't to help her feel better after yesterday's revelations. It was a good business decision, plain and simple.

* * *

Stephanie blinked in disbelief at Blanchard's Run's ownership papers. They'd been delivered to the hotel suite five minutes ago, with her name on the envelope.

She squeezed her eyes shut and shook her head against what had to be an illusion. But, no, she wasn't crazy. That was her name, and Ryder Equestrian Center, and Blanchard's Run's pedigree.

The suite door opened.

Alec strode in and glanced at the papers. A grin spread across his face.

"You?" she asked in amazement.

"I thought you made a convincing case."

She stared up at him, her brain grappling with the situation. "You bought Blanchard's Run?"

He tossed his key card on the table near the foyer. "Was it all true? The EBV thing?"

"Of course it was."

"Good. 'Cause if it's not, I just made a very big mistake."

"It's all true," she assured him with a nod, emotion stinging the backs of her eyes. Nobody had ever trusted her like this before.

"I'll expect him to make money," Alec warned.

She nodded. "He will."

"Are you hungry?"

Suddenly she was. "Starved."

"You want to go out or stay in?"

"Could we eat out on the balcony?" she asked, warm feelings for Alec blossoming inside her. It was a gorgeous night, and she loved the view across the grounds to the arena. She felt like celebrating. And she felt like being alone with Alec.

"I'll call room service," he offered.

"I'm going to shower." She hugged the ownership papers to her chest, smiling all the way to her bedroom.

Alec had made a business investment in her. He trusted her to make good decisions, to make money.

She set the papers carefully on the bedroom desk, smoothing them out. Then she stripped off her work-worn clothes and headed for the shower.

She scrubbed her hair and rinsed it with conditioner. Then she shaved her legs and used some of the rose scented shower gel and body lotion provided by the hotel. After blow-drying, she wrapped herself in a fluffy robe and wandered back into her bedroom.

The windows were open, letting in the fresh night air.

She felt light and happy, optimistic about the future for the first time in weeks. Blanchard's Run would kick Ryder Equestrian Center to a whole new level.

She pulled open the dresser drawers. Her choices were limited, but she was in a mood to dress up.

She found a matching set of underwear, white lace panties and a low-cut bra. She pushed a pair of pearl earrings into her ears, fastened the matching necklace and bracelet, then crossed to the closet for the single dress she'd brought along on the trip.

A soft, clingy knit, it had narrow straps, a low square-cut neck and crisscrossed ties decorating a tapered V back. The skirt flared over her hips, cascading softly toward her knees. She quickly realized the bra wouldn't work and tossed it back in the drawer.

In the bathroom, she put on a little makeup. She tied her hair up, then brushed it back down, then twisted it in a messy knot at the back of her head, letting wisps curl across her forehead and along her temples.

She heard a knock on the suite's outer door. Alec's footfalls told her he was answering, and she gave the waiter a few minutes to finish setting up. Then she slipped her feet into little black sandals and left the bedroom.

Alec wasn't in sight, but the glow of candlelight flickered through the glass, balcony door.

She wandered outside to find hurricane lamps decorating the patterned, white, wrought-iron tables. Linen and silverware was set out, and plump, peach colored cushions softened the chairs. Salad had been served, while a low wreath of flowers surrounded the glass chimney candle at the center of the table.

"Madame?" came a low voice as a tuxedoed waiter appeared.

He pulled out her chair as Alec arrived in the doorway.

He'd also showered and shaved. He wore charcoal slacks and an open collared, white, dress shirt.

His gaze took in her outfit. "You look very nice." The words were reserved, but there was a burn in his eyes that warmed her from head to toe.

She sat down, and Alec took the chair opposite.

The waiter poured them each a glass of ice water to go with their salads, then melted away, closing the glass door behind him as a chorus of crickets ebbed and flowed from the shrubs and grass far below.

"Do my brothers know you bought Blanchard's Run?" She tried a bite of the fresh greens, avocado and raspberry vinaigrette salad.

Alec shook his head, tasting the salad himself. "You can surprise them."

"They'll be very surprised."

Alec shrugged. "It's your horse, your stable."

She took a few more bites, then dared a personal question. "How did you afford him?" She loved the horse, but she didn't want Alec going out on a limb financially.

He stared levelly at her.

"I'm sorry," she quickly apologized. "Was that too personal?"

"No. It just hadn't occurred to me that you didn't know."

"Know what?"

"Anything about my financial status."

"Or your family. Well, except for that little bit about your parents."

"Where I know pretty much everything about you."

She set down her fork. "More than me, as it turns out."

He gave a rueful smile.

The waiter reappeared, removing their salad plates and replacing them with chicken and pasta before disappearing once again.

"Financially I'm perfectly comfortable," said Alec.

Stephanie wasn't sure what that meant.

"I didn't have to borrow money to buy Blanchard's Run," he elaborated.

"So, you didn't marry me for my money?"

He smiled at her. "I didn't marry you for your money."

She cut into the tender chicken. "You know, we never signed a prenup."

"Are you worried?"

"Not anymore," she deadpanned.

"You could come out ahead on this," he speculated.

"Good to know. Since I have very expensive taste in horses."

Alec coughed out a laugh, and she smiled along with

him. His slate eyes reflected the glint of the candlelight, and the flicker of the flame bounced off the planes and angles of his face. He was a spectacularly handsome man.

Her gaze was drawn to his open collar, pushing her thoughts to his muscled chest and impressive shoulders. She couldn't help but remember him naked, in the pale light of her bedroom, his touch, his scent, his taste.

She moved on to his hands, stilled now on the silverware that rested against his plate. The things those hands had done to her.

"Is Madame finished?" The waiter's voice startled her.

"Yes, please." She drew a ragged breath, shifting in her chair as she became aware of the prickled heat chafing her skin.

"We'll skip dessert," Alec told the man. "Thank you for your time."

"Very good, sir." Once more, he disappeared, this time leaving the suite. They were alone.

A full minute of silence ticked by while the breeze freshened, and candlelight flicked across the planes and angles of Alec's face.

"You bought me a horse," she sighed, still not quite believing it could be true.

He shrugged. "I know most guys go with flowers."

"But you're not most guys."

"I guess not."

"*Definitely* not."

He bunched his napkin and tossed it on the table. "So, what did you get me?"

"I was supposed to buy a gift?" She feigned alarm.

He nodded. "It *is* our anniversary."

"What anniversary is that?"

"Fifteen days."

"Ahh," she nodded. "The little known fifteen-day horse-themed anniversary."

"Celebrated from Iceland to Estonia."

"We're in Kentucky."

"So, no present for me?"

She tucked her hair behind her ears. "I saw a ten-gallon hat in the gift shop downstairs."

He grinned. "Not my style."

"A silver, long-horn steer belt buckle?"

He rose from his chair. "Try again."

"I've got a nice riding crop in the trailer."

"Did you mean that to be sexy?"

"Noooo," she chuckled as she shook her head.

"Thank goodness." He made his way around the table. "I mean, *ouch*."

"You'd prefer sexy underwear to leather?"

He held out his hand. "Sexy underwear would definitely be my first choice for a gift."

She placed her hand in his, taking a deep breath and screwing up her courage. "Had to go without a bra tonight," she confessed.

His gaze dipped down. "Guess that saves me some unwrapping."

She rose to her feet, heart pounding, perspiration beginning to glow on her skin. "Yes, it does."

"I've missed you," he said.

"I'm right here," she parroted.

He smiled at the joke. "That's not what I meant." And his gaze did a tour of her body. His eyes darkened to pewter, going molten with desire.

"It's not what I meant, either," she whispered, zeroing in

on his lips, coming up on her toes, while his hand wrapped around to the small of her back and drew her close.

She stroked her palms up the length of his chest, reveling in the play of muscles beneath the thin cotton. She curved over his shoulders, to the back of his neck, into the rough texture of his hairline, while his mouth slowly descended to hers.

She parted her lips, her entire body softening in reaction to her nearness, his touch.

He stopped, lips a fraction of an inch from hers. "Tell me this isn't gratitude."

"Would it matter?" she couldn't resist asking.

"I know I should say yes." He sucked in a breath. "But, honestly. Maybe."

"It's quid pro quo," she teased.

"Sex with you is worth a million dollars?"

She drew back. "Sex? I thought we were talking about a kiss."

"We can stop at a kiss," he assured her, settling his arms more comfortably around her waist.

"I think we should do that," she responded.

"You're lying."

"Absolutely." She inched back, pasting a sultry smile on her face and sliding one of her straps off her shoulder. Then she pushed down the other. The slinky fabric caught on her hardened nipples, clinging there in the candlelight.

Alec glanced around, obviously confirming they had privacy. Then he drew her into the shadow of the overhang.

"For a million dollars," he whispered, as his lips finally came down on hers in an explosion of taste and texture. He kissed her deeply and thoroughly, and her body nearly melted when his fingers found her zipper and pushed it down.

Her dress fell away, the breeze of the night caressing her skin. He surrounded her near naked body with his strong arms, hands roaming everywhere as he pressed her against the smooth, warm concrete wall.

She squirmed against him.

And his breathing rasped. "For a million dollars, I think we're going to have to do it twice."

Twice turned out to be essential for Alec. Because the first time was over far too fast. And he was convinced he could make love to Stephanie all night long.

In his bedroom now, he kissed the damp skin at the back of her neck, drawing her heated body more solidly into the cradle of his own. She fit perfectly. Everything about her fit perfectly, and he was beginning to wonder if he'd ever grow tired of holding her in his arms.

"Tell me about your family," she said softly, toying with the sheet he'd drawn over them both. The comforter had long since hit the floor, and most of the pillows were scattered around the room.

"Not a good time," he breathed. He wanted to focus on here and now, not on the past, and not on the future.

She eased onto her back. "Why not?"

He gazed down at her incredibly gorgeous face. There were two freckles nearly merged together on the cheekbone below her right eye. He kissed them, loving that he was close enough to observe that and so many other intimate and delightful things about her.

"Alec?" she prompted as his hand slid over her hipbone, wandering down her thigh.

"What?"

"Why not?"

He drew back a few inches. "Let me see... Maybe because I've got a beautiful, naked woman in my arms?"

"We already made love."

"We're doing it twice, remember? You insisted."

"I need a rest."

"Liar."

She grinned but didn't give in. "You have to tell me something about your family."

"I was an only child, and my father was a hard-ass."

"How so?"

"He was harsh and demanding, with expectations that nobody could ever hope to meet." Alec kissed her ear, letting his fingertips flutter over her flat stomach.

It blew him away to think of his baby in there. It also blew him away to have her in his bed again. He'd slept with plenty of women, but he'd never felt this close to any of them. And he'd never felt so protective and so completely privileged.

"Did he hurt you?" she asked in a small voice.

Alec drew back again. "You mean physically?"

She nodded.

"Of course he did. But I was a teenager by then, and I could take it."

Her eyes widened in sympathy, and she wrapped her arms around his neck, squeezing tight.

"I love the effect," he told her, hugging her back. "But I'm not crazy about the motivation."

"Oh, Alec."

"Don't do this, Stephanie. It was a long time ago. It wasn't that bad, certainly nothing to turn into a movie of the week."

"Nobody ever hit me," she told him.

His hug tightened reflexively. "They'd better not have."

"It's not fair."

"Nothing's fair. But I got the girl in the end, so I win."

It was her turn to draw back. "You mean me?"

"Who *else* would I mean? How bad do you think I am at this?"

That coaxed a smile out of her. "You mean pillow talk?"

"Like I'm going to lay in bed with you and talk about some other woman."

She shrugged. "How should I know?"

Her question brought a warm glow to his chest. "I love it that I was the first."

"You didn't seem that thrilled at the time."

"I was feeling freaking guilty at the time."

The sympathy was gone from her eyes, and the teasing light was back. "For taking advantage of my innocence?"

"For not having properly appreciated the privilege of being your first lover."

"What about your mother?" she asked.

"You're not going to let this go, are you?"

"No."

He hesitated for a long moment. But Stephanie deserved to know the truth. "She died when I was ten."

Her eyes clouded. "Oh, no. What happened?"

This time, Alec's hesitation was even longer. "She swallowed a bottle of sleeping pills."

Stephanie's eyes went wide. "She killed herself?"

He nodded. "Very few people know that."

Stephanie shook her head to assure him she'd keep the secret. "Do you know why?"

"My father was a hard-ass," Alec repeated.

She closed her eyes and drew him close. "Oh, Alec."

"It was a long time ago." It truly was. "I don't even know why I told you."

"Quid pro quo," she whispered against his shoulder, kissing him softly. "You know all my secrets."

"I do." He skimmed his hand over her belly, along her thighs and around to cup her bottom, feeling so incredibly lucky to be so close to her. "Have I ever told you how grateful I am that you'll be my baby's mother?"

She drew back, giving him an astonished gaze. "Seriously?"

"Seriously." He hesitated.

"Why?" she finally whispered.

He gave in to complete honesty. "Because you're everything I'm not."

Her eyes went round, and he bent to kiss her smooth stomach.

"You hear that, kid?" His voice unexpectedly thickened. "You're going to have the best mother in the world."

She stroked her fingers through his hair, and he kissed her again, softly and leisurely. Then he pecked and suckled his way over her stomach to her breasts. She gasped as he took one pebbled nipple into his mouth, and his body instantly reacted to her taste and texture. Stephanie arched her back, and a small groan came from her lips.

He slipped an arm beneath the small of her back, moving to the other breast, while his hand went on an exploration of its own. After long minutes, he kissed his way to her mouth. She tasted sweet, hauntingly familiar, and he battled a dread of letting her go.

He thrust his tongue into her mouth, feeling a desperation

to brand her as his own, wanting the memory of tonight to be seared indelibly into both of their brains.

She kissed him back, deeply and thoroughly, her palms sliding down his back, over his buttocks, along his thighs. He didn't want to rush her, but the urge to push inside grew stronger and stronger.

Then he felt her thighs twitch. They eased apart, welcoming him. It was all he could do to fight the freight train of desire as instinct took over, and his hips automatically flexed forward.

She bent her knees and rose to meet him, the heat of their bodies searing against each other. He drew his head back, watching her wide eyes as he slowly eased inside. Her cheeks were flushed, her dark lips parted in small gasps, and her pupils dilated as she stared deep into his soul.

He stilled, his voice a rasp. "I could do this forever."

"Please do."

"Oh, yeah."

He watched her intently, while his need built, and the tension in his muscles coiled to painful. Still, he refused to move. A single movement would be the beginning of the end. And he didn't want this to end. He quite literally wanted to stay right here for the rest of his life.

"Oh, Alec," she moaned, and a lightning flash of lust shot through him.

"I know." He held fast.

But her eyes fluttered shut, and her hips flexed forward, and her legs wrapped around him, catapulting his subconscious into action. There was nothing he could do to stop the long strokes of pleasure propelling them forward.

Her nails dug into his back. Her gasps were music to his ears. He inhaled her scent, reveled in her hot, moist core, guiding them both as long and as high as he could manage. Then her cries rocked his world, and her body convulsed against him, and his name on her lips sent him over the edge into rhythmic paradise.

Nine

The scattered showers of the new day made the jump course heavy and less than ideal. But Rosie-Joe had excelled in worse conditions than this.

"Make sure you give her time to get her footing before the triple combination," Stephanie told Wesley.

He was dressed, pressed, trimmed and ready to go, his round coming up in only minutes.

"The rain won't spook her," Stephanie continued. "Keep her balanced, and she should run clean. Just keep your head in the game."

Wesley nodded, his gaze suddenly focusing on something in the distance. A smile grew on his face that seemed just a little too confident.

"Are you listening to me?" she asked, as horses, grooms and competitors shifted around them. The announcer's voice was clear on the PA. The crowd applauded as Bill Roauge and Zepher made it cleanly over the water jump.

"You worry too much."

"Wesley—"

He leaned in close, brushing her arm. "Just wish me luck," he whispered. Then he brushed something from her cheek and tucked her hair behind one ear.

Suddenly a blur of movement crossed her vision. Alec's big hand wrapped around Wesley's arm. Wesley staggered backward, as Alec propelled him ten feet to stop abruptly against the wall.

Stephanie was too stunned to move.

Had Alec lost his mind?

She couldn't see his face, and she couldn't hear his words. But she could see the set of his shoulders, and the width of his stance, and his hand was clamped tight around Wesley's arm. Wesley's cockiness turned to shock, while most of the blood seemed to drain from his face.

The groom holding Rosie-Jo stared in stupefaction, while Stephanie finally spurred herself to action, marching across the floor.

"Do you understand?" Alec ground out in a harsh voice she'd never heard before.

Wesley gave a rapid nod, and before Stephanie could say anything, he broke away from Alec and brushed past her.

She turned, torn between going after him and demanding answers from Alec. But Wesley was already mounting Rosie-Jo, and she couldn't think of a single thing to say to him that might help. So, she rounded on Alec.

"What is the matter with you?" she hissed, moving close to face him.

"Not a single thing."

She gestured to Wesley. "He's about to ride."

"So what?"

"You've completely blown his concentration."

Alec pasted her with a hard stare. "He should have thought of that before coming on to another man's wife."

"What?" she sputtered. What on earth was Alec's problem? After last night, how could he possibly think she had any interest in Wesley?

"You going to watch him?" Alec grimly nodded to where Wesley was entering the ring.

She had to watch.

Of course she had to watch.

"We are not through here," she warned Alec.

"We never are," he sighed as she turned for the fence.

Alec fell into step beside her.

"What are you doing?" she asked.

"I'm coming with you."

"It's probably better if you—"

"This isn't negotiable, Stephanie."

"Then at least stop scowling."

They stopped at the fence as Rosie-Jo cleared the first jump.

"He wasn't coming onto me," she muttered in an undertone.

"I agree," said Alec.

And she turned to him with frank astonishment.

"He was testing *me*," said Alec.

The crowd cheered as Rosie-Joe cleared the next jump.

"Testing you for *what?* You were there last night, Alec. You already won." She reflexively scrutinized Wesley's lineup for the vertical.

"To see what I'd do if he made a move on you. He saw

me coming, Stephanie. He looked me straight in the eyes, launched that smug grin and moved in on you."

Stephanie clearly remembered Wesley's touch and his whisper. "I had dirt on my cheek," she defended.

"No, you didn't. You had a husband within eyeshot and a young pup looking to test the waters."

The crowd cheered again.

"You're paranoid." But she had to admit, something had seemed off about Wesley's gesture. And there was no denying he'd been pushing the boundaries with her since she'd told him about being pregnant.

"I'm not paranoid. I'm realistic."

"He knows it's a marriage of convenience," she felt compelled to defend Wesley. It was probably her own fault for not being clear with him three days ago.

"It doesn't matter."

"It does to him."

Butterflies formed in Stephanie's stomach as Rosie-Jo lined up for the triple. She held her breath.

Oxer, vertical, vertical.

He'd done it. Stephanie let out a breath and applauded along with the rest of the crowd.

But on the next jump, Rosie-Jo rubbed a rail.

Stephanie swore under her breath as the announcer acknowledged the fault.

They made the last three jumps clean, their time putting then in eighth place. A respectable showing.

As the pair approached the exit gate, Stephanie and Alec stepped to one side. Alec tossed an arm over her shoulder.

She knew what he was doing, but she also knew it was what she'd signed up for. And, while she wasn't sure Wesley had deliberately taunted Alec, it was probably better if he understood the boundaries up front, particularly while they were working together.

Wesley scrutinized Stephanie. Then his gaze shifted to Alec. It immediately dropped to the ground. She smiled and congratulated him as he passed, but he didn't look up again.

"What did you say to him?" she couldn't help asking Alec.

"That another man would have taken his head off. And he would have."

"I can't believe this has got blown so far out of proportion." She needed to talk to Wesley. The sooner, the better.

"He's a punk kid," said Alec, drawing her further back from the gate, out of the way of the horse and groom traffic, turning to face her. "It's past time for him to learn right from wrong."

"It's partly my fault," she acknowledged. "For telling him we were getting married because of the baby."

Alec's steel gaze burned into hers. "That doesn't change our vows."

"It gave him expectations."

"Are they valid, Stephanie?" The noise of the crowd and loudspeaker disappeared under Alec's intensity.

The question annoyed her. "What do you think?"

"Then tell him."

"I did. I tried. He refuses to understand."

Alec's jaw went hard. "He understands now."

She couldn't help but worry about Wesley. "Did you scare him?"

"Absolutely. And I wasn't bluffing. If he comes near you again—"

"I'm still his coach."

"You know what I mean. And he knows what I mean."

The crowd applauded, and Stephanie glanced behind herself to the board, seeing a new leader. Wesley was bumped to ninth.

She turned back to Alec and heaved a sigh. "This is going to be very complicated."

"No, it's going to be very simple. You'll be professional. He'll be professional. And nobody will get hurt."

"Sometimes you sound like my brothers."

Alec unexpectedly twitched a grin. "That's definitely not what I was going for."

And suddenly last night was between them, as vividly as if they'd had videotape. She remembered his body, the feel, the taste, the sound of his voice and the intimate things they'd said.

It was a crazy situation, a confusing situation. They had one last night before they separated and went back to their individual lives. She hadn't the vaguest idea what would happen to them then. The only thing she knew for sure was that she'd spend this last night with Alec.

In the morning, Alec watched Stephanie preparing to load the Ryder stables trailers on the Brighton grounds. It was overcast, with rain threatening again. He'd pretty much blown his flight out of the Cedarvale Airport, but he didn't care. He was staying right here until she was on the road.

Stephanie had flown in last week, but she was traveling home with the horses, a couple of grooms and Wesley. Alec wasn't crazy about the arrangement, but he was the one who'd bought Blanchard's Run. And now she insisted on accompanying the stallion back to Montana.

She was dressed in blue jeans, scuffed boots and a navy

T-shirt, and he couldn't help but contrast it to the way she'd looked last night. She'd worn a sexy, white nightie—for a short time, anyway. Then they'd made love and retired to the deep whirlpool tub. Afterward, they'd wrapped themselves in the plush robes provided by the hotel.

They'd sat up late on the balcony, talking about family, music, even politics. Anything to avoid the real topic, which was what happened next in their relationship. Afterward, she'd slept in his arms, while he let his imagination explore risky and unlikely scenarios, involving him and Stephanie, and their baby.

He was playing with fire here, and he knew full well somebody could get hurt. He only hoped it was him and not Stephanie.

Rosie-Jo's hooves clanked on the ramp up to the cavernous trailer, while Royce appeared at Alec's side.

"Any updates on the money?" asked Royce.

Alec nodded. "Damien called last night. Since Stephanie knows the truth, our negotiating position has changed, He thinks he can get back a million or two."

"That's it?"

"He thinks Norman Stanton liked women, ponies and high living. There's a house in Miami, a sports car and an astonishingly small bank account."

Royce crossed his arms over his chest. "Not enough to impact the corporation's bottom line."

"Nowhere near," Alec agreed. "But I'll have some final numbers on that for you in my formal report next week."

Royce nodded, glancing at his watch. "You flying out of Cedarvale?"

"I am."

"The Lexington flight leaves from there in forty minutes."

"I'll catch the next one."

"The next one's tomorrow."

Alec shrugged. "I'll get there."

"I've got the jet. You need me to drop you off somewhere?"

There was something odd in Royce's tone, and Alec searched the man's expression.

Was there something he wanted to talk about in private?

Did he have more secrets?

If he did, Alec wished he'd do them both a favor and keep them the hell to himself. The last thing he wanted was to get embroiled in Ryder family politics again.

"I hear you put Wesley into a wall yesterday," said Royce.

"That's an exaggeration."

"Not from what I heard."

"Who'd you hear it from?"

"It wasn't Stephanie."

Alec hadn't thought it was, particularly since he hadn't left her side for nearly twenty-four hours. He did wonder if it was Wesley himself.

"He was out of line," he told Royce.

Royce gave a thoughtful nod. "I know how that goes."

Alec wasn't sure what Royce was getting at. Was he annoyed because Alec had gone after one of their stable clients?

"What did he do?" asked Royce.

He touched her cheek? He touched her hair? Both of those things sounded lame when they were out of context. "None of your business," said Alec.

"Then, tell me something." Royce turned away to watch the Ryder crew, prepping the trailer, widening his stance, stuffing his hands into the front pockets of his blue jeans.

Alec followed his line of vision to where Stephanie was coiling a lead rope. Wesley was packing up the ramps in preparation to leave.

"About my sister." Royce continued, tone thoughtful. "Would you shoot any guy who touched her?"

"In a heartbeat," said Alec.

Royce clicked his cheek. "That's how it starts."

It wasn't exactly a trick question. "Name one guy who wouldn't?"

Royce turned back to Alec. "So, I take it you're going with Plan A."

"Plan A?"

"The one where you make her fall in love with you."

"I'm not going with Plan A." Plan A was fraught with peril.

Then again, he wasn't going with Plan B, either—the one where he disappeared from her life for months at a time.

He hadn't come up with any plan that seemed workable under the circumstance.

"I'm going to say goodbye," he told Royce. Then he left him behind, crossing the small chunk of parking lot that brought him to Stephanie.

"We're about ready to take off," she informed him as he approached, smiling openly, her face scrubbed fresh, her auburn hair flowing in the wind.

"Are you sure you wouldn't rather fly?"

She cocked her head. "Didn't we already have this debate?"

"I wasn't happy with the outcome."

"I'm staying with Blanchard's Run. I'm going to protect your investment."

But his investment wasn't the most valuable thing involved in this package. "You hired his personal groom to take care of him."

"I'm driving to Montana, Alec." Her expression sobered, and her clear blue eyes reflected the gathering clouds. "What about you?"

"Back to Chicago."

She nodded, and her smile came back. It looked a little forced to him, but he couldn't be sure.

"For a week," he elaborated, watching her closely. "Then I'm coming to Montana."

She sobered then swallowed.

"My report will be ready."

"Oh. Right." She gave a little laugh. "Of course."

He wanted to say more. He wanted to tell her he was coming for *her,* not for the damn report. He wanted to tell her they would work this out, that he was falling fast and hard for her, and he was having trouble picturing his life without her.

But it was too soon. And he couldn't risk hurting her. He had no idea how she felt. And half a dozen people were watching them.

He should have asked her last night. But, the truth was, he was afraid of her answer. She'd told Wesley it was a marriage of convenience. And it was. And it might never be anything else.

"See you in Montana?" he asked.

She nodded. See you in Montana.

Ten

Stephanie wished she'd had at least five minutes alone with Alec before the meeting convened around the dining room table at the main ranch house. She's been on the road for days, arriving home last night with Blanchard's Run. Her cell phone conversations with Alec had been sporadic and brief during the long stretches of isolated highway. And there'd been little privacy for evening conversations, since she was sharing motel rooms with the female groom.

She missed him. And she was beginning to doubt her memories. She'd tried to cling to the intimacy they'd shared in Kentucky, but as the days rolled by, she began to fear she'd imagined it.

She'd wanted to talk to him alone before the meeting, but his plane had been late. It was raining hard. And her truck got stuck in the mud on the way down the hill from her place in a pocket where there was no cell signal.

She was the last to arrive. She was wet through to her underwear. Her hair was stringy, and mud caked her boots. Her shower had been a waste of time, and the makeup she'd applied after lunch was long gone. So much for hoping Alec might find her attractive.

"There you are," said Royce as she kicked off her boots in the front hallway.

"Got stuck on Moss Hill," she explained, swiping her hands over her riotous hair, hoping against hope she didn't have mascara running down her cheeks.

"Just got here myself," McQuestin put in, in an obvious attempt to make her feel better.

Stephanie's gaze skipped around the long, rectangular table, Jared, Melissa, Royce, Amber, McQuestin, ah, finally, Alec at one end. The last time she'd seen him here was their wedding. And she couldn't quite contain her smile. He looked so good, immaculate suit, fresh shave, trimmed hair.

He smiled back and gave her a nod, but something about him seemed reserved.

She quickly schooled her features, taking an empty chair halfway down one side.

"Are we ready?" asked Jared where he was positioned at the other end of the table.

There were several nods.

"Then let me start by thanking Alec for his hard work. We know this won't be easy. And we understand we're not going to like everything you have to recommend. But I'd like to say on behalf of my family, that we'll take a serious look at all of your suggestions."

Alec nodded his head in acknowledgment. "I appreciate that, Jared." He shuffled a stack of papers in front of him. "Perhaps I'll start with the ranch." He looked to McQuestin.

"The cattle operation has lost money for several years in a row."

McQuestin screwed up his weathered face, narrowing his eyes.

"However," Alec continued. "Beef prices are on the rise. While land values are at a low. So selling doesn't make sense—"

"'Course it doesn't," said McQuestin.

"With some streamlining to management," Alec continued, "the ranch ought to be able to break even."

"Streamlining?" McQuestin challenged.

"You've stopped paying the blackmail, for starters," said Alec. "And best practices have come a long way in the past thirty years. I'd suggest hiring an agricultural studies grad and—"

"An academic?" McQuestin spat.

"McQuestin," Jared warned. "We said we'd listen."

But Alec was smiling. "Unless you'd like to enroll in college yourself."

McQuestin's bushy brows went up, while everyone else tittered with laughter.

"The details are in my report." Alec flipped a page. "On to the real estate division. As I'm sure you're all aware, it's had the highest profitability for the past few years. But that's about to be challenged. Rental rates are on a downward trend in Chicago, and vacancies are expected to rise."

Stephanie glanced at Jared, but his expression gave away nothing.

"You have a couple of choices there," said Alec. "Ride it out, or sell off either or both of the Maple Street and industrial properties. I'd absolutely recommend keeping everything you've got in the downtown core. When the market recovers, that will go up first."

Jared nodded, but didn't venture an opinion.

"*Windy City Bizz* magazine," said Alec. "Sell that puppy just as fast as you can."

Royce sat up straight. "No. That's Amber's—"

"No, Royce." Amber put her hand on his shoulder. "You should sell it."

"There's no saving print publications," said Alec. "Particularly periodicals."

Stephanie drew a sigh, gauging Amber's expression. She looked sad, but not hugely upset. Stephanie, on the other hand, was getting more uncomfortable by the minute.

Ryder International had been a strong and growing company for as long as she could remember. Jared was an amazing entrepreneur, and Royce seemed to excel at acquisitions. She couldn't quite believe they were in this much trouble.

"What about the jet?" asked Royce, tension evident around his mouth.

"You're going to need it," said Alec. "I know it feels like an indulgence, but you've got interests in half a dozen states. You need to be mobile."

Amber gave Royce's arm a squeeze.

"On the legal issues with your father's will." Alec's gaze flicked to Stephanie for a split second. "I'd recommend vesting Stephanie with nonvoting shares."

Stephanie was sure she couldn't have heard right.

"She doesn't have time to pay attention to the corporate issues—"

"Wait a minute," Stephanie blurted out. She glanced from Jared to Royce, and then to Alec. "You don't want me to vote?"

"I don't want you to *have* to vote. There are a myriad of things that you—"

"How is that different?" What was the matter with him? How could he have blindsided her like that?

He directed his next words to Jared. "You and Royce should have an equal partnership. Frame up a dispute resolution process if necessary, but don't make Stephanie the swing vote."

"Wait a minute," Stephanie shouted.

Jared shot her a look. "We'll give it some thought."

"How can you—"

"Stephanie," Jared warned. "We can discuss it later."

She compressed her lips then turned her cold glare from Jared to Alec. "It's a stupid idea."

"Steph," Royce put in kindly. "You can convince us of that later."

"Fine," she huffed. Her brothers would never go for it anyway. She might only be a half sister, but they loved her. They wouldn't strip away her power for no reason.

What was *wrong* with Alec? What could have changed between the time he bought her Blanchard's Run and now?

"High tech is the future," said Alec. "I wouldn't recommend selling, but you might want to look at some international licensing deals. You can maximize your sales without growing the division to an unwieldy size."

Nobody answered to that.

"On sports and culture." Alec flipped a page in front of him. "I'd suggest standing pat."

Stephanie blew out a sigh. It wasn't relief. It was, well, okay, it was relief.

"Except for the jumping stable."

She stilled, feeling all gazes land on her.

"It's a cash drain, and there's no end in sight." He looked up, taking Stephanie in along with everyone else, pausing no longer, no shorter on her stunned expression than on any of the others. "You need to sell off the entire operation. The sooner the better."

Stephanie found her voice. "Wait just a—"

"May I please finish?" he cut in.

"No, you may not finish. You've just recommended selling something that I spent half my life—"

"Stephanie—"

"—building!" She came to her feet.

"I don't expect you to—"

"How could you *do* this?"

"Will you have a little faith?"

"No. I will not." She rapped her knuckles down on the polished tabletop. "Is there any part of my life you're *not* planning to destroy?"

Alec's lips compressed, eyes darkening to pinpoints.

Stephanie turned on Jared. "Since I have no voting privileges, I guess you two can do whatever you want. But I'm not going to sit around and listen to this guy pick over our family like a vulture."

"Stephanie," Royce tried.

"No!" She turned on her second brother, backing up, scraping her chair legs against the wood floor as she pushed it out of the way. Then she pivoted on her stocking feet and stalked for the door, grabbing her muddy boots on the way out.

"Excuse me," Alec's voice intoned to the group behind her as she slammed the door.

She quickly stuffed her foot into the first boot. Then hopped in place on the porch as she struggled with the other.

The door opened and Alec stepped out. "What the hell is the matter with you?"

"With me? With *me?*" She rammed her foot down to the sole, straightening and flipping her hair over her shoulder. "You're the one out to destroy my life."

He folded his arms over his chest. "You are rushing to preposterous conclusions."

She leaned in. "Tell me one thing, Alec. Why did you buy me Blanchard's Run?"

"Why do you think I bought you Blanchard's Run?"

She gave the only plausible answer she'd come up with. "Because you felt guilty."

"It was not guilt."

"Why then?" she rattled on. "So I'd sleep with you?"

He sputtered out a cold laugh. "Yeah, right."

She forced a note of contempt into her voice. "Well, congratulations, Alec. It worked. I slept with you because you bought me a horse."

"No, you didn't."

"Oh, yes, I did." She glared straight at him, and his eyes flickered with uncertainty.

"What?" she asked sarcastically. "Did you think I'd fallen for your good looks, wit and charm? Think again, Alec. I wanted the horse. You got me the horse. I figured I owed you. And since we'd done it once already—"

"Stop it."

"Truth hurts?"

"Lies hurt, Stephanie."

"Yeah. They do. And we've been a lie from minute one. I'm sorry I forgot about that."

She nodded toward the door behind Alec. "Better get back to your job. My brothers can let me know what they decide." Then she turned, searching for every scrap of dignity she could muster as she paced down the stairs.

As Alec reentered the house, the faces staring at him from the dining room table alternated between condemnation and frank curiosity.

"We stopped them from going after her," Amber informed him.

"I'm sure you did." Alec could well have imagined Jared and Royce's first reaction was to rush outside and save their sister from him. "Thank you," he finished, including both Amber and Melissa in his gratitude.

"We're not selling the jumping stable," Royce informed him, clearly ticked off.

Alec shook his head in disgust. When he'd planned his little speech, he'd planned it all the way to the end, where he revealed his master plan and became Stephanie's hero. He hadn't counted on her being so dogged in her interruptions. And he sure hadn't counted on hearing such a painful truth about her feelings for him.

He'd been looking forward to getting back to Montana from the minute he left Stephanie at Brighton. Now all he wanted to was get the hell out of the state.

He dropped back into his chair. "I want you to sell the jumping stable to *me*."

They all blinked at him in silence.

He threw up his hands, spelling it out in detail. "I'm married to Stephanie. It'll be half hers. This way, Ryder International won't be stuck with the financial liability, but she'll still—"

"Did you tell that to Stephanie?" Amber asked.

He glared at her but didn't answer the question. "I can afford the cash drain. I'll be a silent partner."

Jared snorted. "That's why you don't want her to have voting shares in Ryder International."

"She's going to be a little busy with other interests," said Alec. That, and he'd selfishly assumed she might want a little time left over for him.

"You need to tell her," said Melissa.

"So she'll be grateful?" His voice was sharper than he intended, and Jared frowned at him.

"Sorry," Alec apologized. "You all know my marriage to Stephanie is a sham—"

"Say what?" McQuestin seemed to come back to life.

"She's pregnant," said Alec, not willing to keep any more secrets.

"And you did the right thing?" asked McQuestin, lined face screwing up as he narrowed his eyes, sizing up Alec as if he was debating getting his shotgun. A little late for that.

"I did the right thing," Alec confirmed. "I'll live up to my responsibility, including providing for her and my child by buying and financing the Ryder Equestrian Center. But there's nothing more than that between us."

"Are you sure?" asked Amber.

"Positive," said Alec.

Royce looked to Jared. "Yeah. Except that he'll shoot any man who touches her."

Jared's eyebrows shot up, and he turned his attention to Alec. "You poor bastard."

"What?" asked Melissa.

"It's a joke," said Royce. "A bad joke."

"Explain," demanded Amber.

Alec gathered his paperwork. Jared and Royce's pity was the final straw. If a man had to have his heart broken, he could at least do it in private. "I'll leave a copy of my recommendations for your review. You are, of course, welcome to use or discard anything."

"Explain," Melissa echoed.

Jared gave in. "You know, when Dad murdered Frank Stanton—"

McQuestin rocked forward. *"What?"*

Royce jumped in. "It's a barometer of how much you love your wife."

"Alec's in love with Stephanie?" asked Melissa.

"Alec is saying goodbye," said Alec, turning for the door.

McQuestin jumped into the fray. "Your father didn't murder Frank Stanton."

Everybody went silent and stared at McQuestin. Even Alec froze then turned back.

"It was self-defense," said the old man. "Your mother had changed her mind. She refused to leave with Stanton. Stanton got mad and shot at your dad. He hit your mother by accident in the shoulder, and your father shot back. Your father was rushing her to the hospital when the truck went into the river."

"Then why did Gramps hide the gun?" asked Jared.

"Make it look like a robbery." McQuestin gave him a stern look. "Trials are unpredictable."

And the affair would have been public knowledge. Alec didn't agree with the action, but he thought he understood the motivation. Still, it didn't change anything for him. His hope of a future with Stephanie was over. The sooner he got back to Chicago, the better.

The room went silent as everyone digested the revelation.

"I've got a plane to catch," Alec put in. He didn't exactly

have a ticket, since he'd been hoping to stay here with Stephanie. But nobody needed to know that.

"If you leave," Amber ventured, cocking her head sideways. "How are you going to shoot any man who touches her?"

"Nobody's shooting anyone," he returned. And Stephanie didn't want or need his protection.

Royce came to his feet. "You're just going to abandon her?"

"What part of marriage of convenience don't you understand?"

"The part where you fell in love with my sister."

Alec opened his mouth to deny it, but he found he couldn't lie. There was no point in even attempting to salvage his pride. "She doesn't love me."

"Are you sure?" asked Amber.

Alec gave a sharp nod.

"Then change her mind," Jared put in mildly. "Melissa didn't start off loving me."

Royce grinned. "And Amber took some convincing."

Amber socked him in the arm. "I loved you, dummy. I just didn't tell you about it."

It was painful for Alec to watch the interplay. "It's better if I just leave."

"You sure?" McQuestin put in gruffly, his pale gaze boring into Alec. "Because if you're wrong, and you break that little girl's heart. *I'm* the one who'll be shooting at *you.*"

Two miles from the main ranch, Stephanie jerked her car to the side of the muddy road and brought it to an abrupt halt.

Her hands were shaking. Her stomach ached. And she

couldn't seem to muster up enough strength in her leg to push the clutch and gear down for the hill.

What was she going to do?

She'd come home with such high hopes. But the days and nights at Brighton now seemed like a cruel dream. She'd fallen fast and hard for her husband, and it had seemed like he was falling for her. She'd even dared to hope it was love.

But he didn't love her. He didn't even like or respect her. Why else would he have stripped away her business?

There had to have been other options.

Why was it *her* who had to sacrifice everything?

She gripped the steering wheel, her anger reviving, blocking out her heartache.

But then she remembered *Windy City Bizz*. Amber loved that magazine. Yet, she'd quickly agreed to sell it. And Royce had offered up the jet. And Jared had spent years building up their Chicago property inventory. He had huge plans for construction in the next decade, yet he was looking at selling.

Stephanie swallowed, a horrible thought creeping into her mind. Had she just let her brothers down? Was this why they kept secrets from her? Did they think she couldn't handle the hard truths?

She sat back, shoulders drooping, considering for the first time in her life that she might have some responsibility to turn a financial profit, not just to provide theoretical PR and goodwill. She had an obligation to her family. And she had an obligation to Alec.

Another ranch truck rocked to a halt beside her. But she didn't even look up.

Moments later, Amber banged on the window.

"Stephanie!"

Stephanie blinked blankly at Amber. Her pride was in tatters and her heart was broken to bits.

She loved Alec.

She realized he wasn't trying to hurt her. He was trying to treat her like an adult, a functioning partner. He'd done her the courtesy of telling her the hard truth about her stable, instead of trying to sugarcoat it so she wouldn't get hurt.

She loved him, and he respected her. And she'd just destroyed any chance they might have had at building a future together.

"Will you open—" Amber grabbed the door handle and yanked the driver's door wide. "You have to come back."

Stephanie shook her head. She couldn't go back. She was mortified by her behavior, and she needed to go home and bury her head.

"He's leaving," Amber rushed on. "He's leaving now. McQuestin threatened to shoot him, but he's still leaving."

"What?" Stephanie managed to say, completely confused by Amber's agitation.

"Stephanie." Amber took a breath. "Listen to me. Alec wanted to sell the stable—"

"He was right," Stephanie nodded, swallowing her pain.

"—to *himself.*"

Stephanie struggled to make sense of the words.

"*He* was going to buy it. *You* were going to run it. Hell, you were going to own half of it, since you're his wife."

Stephanie felt the blood drain from her face, while the roar of a hurricane pounded in her ears.

Amber grabbed her hand, tugging on it. "You have to come back. *Now.*"

Stephanie fumbled with her seat belt catch. "I don't understand."

"He loves you."

"Who loves me?" Stephanie pushed off the seat, landing on the muddy road.

"Alec. He loves you."

Stephanie didn't believe that for a minute. And even if he had, he didn't anymore. Still a little part of her heart couldn't help holding out hope. "He said that?" she dared ask as Amber bundled her into the passenger seat of the other truck.

"He said he'd shoot any man who touched you." Amber swung into the driver's side and put the truck in gear.

"That's not exactly the same thing," Stephanie pointed out.

"It's some kind of a joke. But Royce says it means he loves you. But he's convinced you don't love him. And he's heading for the airport. From there, with his job, who knows where he'll end up." Amber glanced across the seat, voice lowering. "So, if you love him, Stephanie…"

Stephanie stared back. She slowly nodded.

"You need to tell him. And you need to do it right now."

"I'm sorry," Stephanie mumbled. "I wasn't thinking. You gave up the magazine. Royce offered the jet. Of course I'll give up the stable. I didn't mean to sound so spoiled and selfish back there."

Amber unexpectedly smiled. "Me giving up the magazine is nothing compared to you giving up the stable. Your brothers were never going to let that happen. Of course, as it turns out, that wasn't what Alec meant anyway."

"He wants to *buy* the stable?" Stephanie turned the revelation over in her mind.

"And he made it clear you'd be half owner. And he'd be a silent partner. And he was doing it to provide for his wife and his child."

"Oh, no." Acute regret slid through Stephanie's stomach.

"But it's good news."

Stephanie blew out a sigh. "I said some things. To Alec. When I thought he was out to get me."

"What things?"

Stephanie groaned. "He must hate me."

"What things?"

"That I only slept with him the second time—"

"You slept with him a second time?"

"And a third and a fourth and a fifth. Maybe more. I kind of lost count."

Amber laughed. "Well, that sounds promising."

"No." Stephanie shook her head. "I just finished telling him I'd only done it because he bought Blanchard's Run. It was gratitude sex, and I didn't find him either handsome, funny or charming. I may have said I didn't like him. I definitely implied he should get lost."

"Do you think he believed you?"

"I was pretty convincing."

"But you're in love with him?"

Stephanie moaned, bending forward around her stomachache. "Yes."

"Maybe try telling him that." The truck rocked to a halt. Stephanie looked up to see Jared, Melissa, Royce and McQuestin standing in the front driveway.

She glanced frantically around for Alec, opening the door, stepping out.

"He's gone," said Jared.

"How long?" asked Amber.

"Twenty minutes, at least." Royce shook his head.

"I'm going after him," Stephanie decided. Amber was right. While Stephanie had been dead wrong. She owed him an apology, and she was going to suck up her pride and tell him she loved him.

She was sure it would be nothing but a lesson in abject humiliation, because no man was going to love a woman who'd behaved the way she did. And despite his joke to Royce, she was sure Alec would be happy to put as much distance as possible between himself and her.

She looked to Amber. "Give me the keys."

"You'll never catch him," said Melissa. "And it's dangerous to try."

"Take the Cessna," McQuestin put in.

Royce looked at the old man, then grinned. "We'll take the Cessna." He grabbed the keys from Amber and headed to the truck at a trot. "Come on," he called to Stephanie.

She sprinted after him.

It was a five-minute drive to the ranch airstrip. Royce sped through his pre-flight checklist. Stephanie slapped on the earphones and strapped into the seat and braced herself for takeoff.

In no time, they were skimming a thousand feet above the ranch road. The road met the main road, and they banked east. There'd be little traffic before the Interstate, so Alec's black car should be easy to spot.

After they found him? Well, things were definitely going to get tough. She tried to come up with a speech in her mind, something, *anything* that might help him forgive her. But she was drawing a blank.

"Painful, isn't it?" asked Royce through the radio.

"I was so stupid."

He laughed. "We all are. I told Amber she should marry her former fiancé. I could have lost her right then and there."

"But you didn't."

"No, I didn't."

Stephanie peered out the small windshield, scanning the length of road in front of them. Range land whizzed by, with the occasional barn or stream. "We don't know how this one's going to turn out."

"He loves you, Steph."

"I may have killed that."

"You can't kill it. Believe me, you can't kill it."

Stephanie drew a breath, desperately trying to convince herself that Royce knew what he was talking about. But the fact was, he didn't. His and Amber's relationship was unique and special. It wasn't representative of every other relationship in the world.

"There he is," said Royce, pointing to the road. And Stephanie's heart went into overdrive.

Royce overflew the car, checked for traffic, then turned the Cessna in a tight circle, bringing it down on the pavement of the road. They coasted to a stop, and he shut off the engine.

Stephanie removed her headphones, unclipped the harness then clambered out of the small seat, stepping on the wing strut before dropping down to the pavement.

"Go get 'em, tiger," Royce called with an encouraging grin.

Stephanie couldn't muster up a smile in return. Her palms were sweating and her knees were weak. She took a few trembling steps along the centerline, watching for Alec's car to come into view. She didn't have long to wait.

The black car coasted to a stop, but Alec didn't get out.

Squinting, at the tinted windshield, Stephanie forced herself to walk toward it.

Finally the door opened, and Alec stepped out, frowning. "What the hell?"

"I'm sorry, Alec."

He looked at the plane, then back to her. "What the *hell?*"

"It's Royce. We were afraid you'd beat us to the airport and get on a plane, and I wouldn't be able to find you."

"So you landed on the *highway?* Have you lost your mind?"

"I came to apologize."

He was still frowning. His eyes were squinted down in anger. "It never occurred to me in a million years that I'd have to make this rule. But don't you ever, *ever* take my baby up in an airplane and land on a public roadway."

"It's perfectly safe. We checked for traffic."

"Stephanie."

"Okay. Okay. I won't." She paused. "But don't you want to know why I'm here?"

"To say you're sorry?"

She screwed up her courage. "To say I love you."

His expression never flinched. "They told you about me buying the stable?"

She nodded.

"And you're grateful for that?"

"It's not about gratitude."

His look turned skeptical. "Really?"

"It was never about gratitude for Blanchard's Run."

"That's not what you said an hour ago."

"I lied an hour ago."

"But you're not lying now?"

"No."

He took a step forward, jaw clenched, expression grim. "Explain to me, Stephanie. How exactly am I supposed to tell the difference?"

It was a fair question. She moved closer to him. "I guess you can't."

His expression softened ever so slightly. "So, when you tell me that you love me? Which, by the way, I desperately want to believe—"

"But you need proof?" she ventured.

"And it can't be sex."

"Too bad." Her voice dropped low. "I've been thinking about sex all week."

Something twitched in his expression.

"I missed you so much," she told him. "I thought about you all morning. I imagined you pulling me back into your arms, holding me tight, and telling me everything was going to work out for us."

"And instead I threatened to sell your home out from under you."

"I should have listened longer. And it shouldn't have mattered. I should have been able to handle the hard truth."

"I should have started with the punch line."

"I love you, Alec. I don't know how to prove that to you, but I'm willing to do anything you say."

A grin twitched the corners of his mouth. "Marry me?"

"I already did."

He reached out and took her hands in his. "Have my baby? No. Wait. You're already doing that."

She couldn't help but smile.

"And since we're already having amazing sex…" He drew her in closer. "I can't come up with a single thing that would definitively prove you love me."

"I could shoot somebody," Stephanie ventured.

His hand slipped to the back of her neck, fingers burrowing into her hairline. "What are you talking about?"

"Amber said it was some kind of a joke. It meant you loved me."

"I do love you," he admitted, and a heavy weight lifted from Stephanie's chest. "But there'll be no shooting involved."

"Okay by me. Hey, I have an idea."

"Shoot."

She rolled her eyes. "What if we live happily ever after? We pull that off, you can be sure that I love you."

Alec smiled as he leaned in. "Deal." Then his lips came down on hers, and he drew her tightly into the circle of his strong arms.

She pressed her body against him, clinging to him, loving him with ever fiber of her being.

Epilogue

After considering nearly every wedding location on the planet, Amber had finally decided on a casual wedding at the ranch. She and Royce were married in the meadow overlooking Evergreen Falls.

She'd confided in Stephanie that it was as far removed as she could get from a cathedral and a ballroom in Chicago—the plan she'd had in place with her former fiancé, the one who was now married to Katie, her best friend and maid of honor.

It was full on summer, a year since Stephanie had met Alec. Their baby girl was now three months old, and little Heidi had slept the ceremony away in her father's arms. Now she was resting her head on his shoulder, staring wide-eyed at the lively country band that had taken over the deck of the ranch house.

The patio had turned into a dance floor, with the overflow spilling onto the lawn.

"You going to start riding again?" Royce asked Stephanie as he twirled her in his arms to the sweeping strains of a breakup song.

"I just got the okay from the doctor."

"But did you get the okay from Alec?"

Stephanie laughed. "Did you get the okay from Amber to keep flying?"

Her brother frowned.

"Same thing," she pointed out.

"Not exactly."

"Yes, exactly."

"How many times have you fallen off a horse?"

"Dozens," she responded. "Hundreds."

"I rest my case. I've never once fallen out of my airplane."

Stephanie caught the warm gaze of her husband, and he playfully waved Heidi's hand in her direction.

"Alec wants me to ride," she informed her brother.

"Alec wants you to smile. Trust me, he doesn't want you to ride."

"He can't stop me."

"He can get you pregnant again."

"He would nev—" Stephanie frowned. Wait a minute. Was that why he was being so cavalier about birth control?

Royce started to laugh.

Stephanie stopped dancing and drew back from his arms. She turned, eyes narrowing in Alec's direction.

Alec shot back a look of confusion.

"Melissa," Royce sang, drawing his six months pregnant sister-in-law into his arms.

"What did you say to her?" Melissa's laughing voice followed Stephanie to the edge of the patio.

Alec's brows narrowed in confusion, while Heidi gurgled and waved her arms toward Stephanie.

"How many kids do you want?" she asked Alec, retrieving her daughter and settling Heidi against her shoulder.

"As many as I can get," he answered with a grin.

"I'm not giving up riding."

"Huh?"

"You can't keep me pregnant all the time."

"Who says I'm trying to keep you pregnant?"

"Royce."

Alec's gaze shot past her. "Well, what the hell does Royce know?"

She leaned in. "You didn't want to use a condom last night."

Alec lowered his voice. "You're still breast-feeding."

"It's not foolproof."

"Nothing's foolproof."

"I'm jumping Rosie-Jo tomorrow," she warned.

"Go for it. I'll baby-sit."

"Really?"

"Yes, really. And stop listening to your brother. He's trying to stir up trouble."

Stephanie glanced to where her brother had switched dance partners once more. He now held his bride, Amber, in his arms, her gauzy white dress flowing around the satin slippers on her feet. He whispered something in her ear, and she smacked him in the shoulder. He just grinned and winked.

That was her brother Royce, all right, stirring up trouble.

"I think our princess is tuckered out," said Alec,

smoothing his hand over Heidi's silky hair as her mouth stretched in a wide yawn.

Stephanie smiled. "Home?"

"Home." He nodded.

She turned and caught Amber's gaze, giving her a little wave.

Amber mouthed, "thank you," keeping her head tucked against Royce's shoulder. They'd see each other for a proper goodbye in the morning before the couple left on their honeymoon.

"Want me to take her?" asked Alec as they made their way toward the stairs to the deck. Through the house was the fastest way to the driveway and their truck.

"I'm fine," Stephanie answered, starting up the short staircase while Alec kept close behind.

Heidi's warm little body relaxed into sleep, even as they passed the drummer.

"Keys in the truck?" asked Alec as they crossed the living room.

"Should be." Stephanie snagged a final cheese puff from the buffet on the dining room table.

"You're *still* hungry?" Alec teased.

"You try feeding a baby." She took two steps back and washed the cheese puff down with a strawberry.

Alec pulled open the front door and stood aside to let her pass.

"Thank you, sir," she mocked as she sashayed through.

"I just like the view from—" Alec nearly barreled into the back of her where she'd frozen still on the top step.

"Hello, Alec." Damien gave him a nod.

But Stephanie's gaze was fixed on the man standing next

to Damien. He was older, clean shaven, his jawline softer, face wrinkled and shoulders stooped.

The front door banged open to Royce's jovial voice. "You trying to sneak—" Royce stopped, too. Then a lighter set of footsteps came to a halt on the porch.

"Stanton," Royce growled.

Alec stepped around Stephanie and Heidi, putting his body between her and Norman Stanton.

"We'd hoped the party would be over," Damien apologized.

"What the hell arc you doing?" Alec demanded of his friend.

Royce took a step forward, coming parallel with Alec, while Jared appeared out of nowhere.

Norman Stanton cleared his throat. "I'm sorry—"

"You're *sorry?*" Royce roared.

Norman swallowed convulsively, and Stephanie found herself pitying the man.

"I didn't mean to intrude."

"This is my *wedding*."

"I knew you were leaving tomorrow," said Damien, stepping forward to hand Royce an envelope.

Alec stepped up to Damien, voice low. "Start talking."

Norman spoke up. "I never meant to hurt any of you."

Jared stepped forward. "If you're not hightailing it off Ryder land in about thirty seconds, you're the one who's getting hurt."

"It was Clifton," said Norman.

"Don't you *dare* speak my father's name."

"Damien?" Alec warned in another undertone.

"I thought he murdered Frank!" Norman all but wailed.

Everyone stilled, and Stephanie found herself mes-merized by the pain in the older man's eyes.

"He was my brother. And he was murdered. And I went after revenge."

Stephanie glanced at her brothers to see them exchange a look.

"I told him the truth," said Damien.

"I know now that it was self-defense," Norman clarified. He peered between Alec and Royce, seeking out Stephanie's gaze. "He loved your mother."

Alec stepped sideways, blocking Norman's view.

"And he loved you."

"Don't you speak to my wife," said Alec.

Stephanie touched Alec's arm. "It's okay."

Alec didn't move. "No, it's not."

Royce's incredulous voice rang out. "This is *ten million dollars.*"

Stephanie turned to see the envelope flutter to the ground.

"I wanted to pay you back," said Norman.

"I helped him liquidate," Damien put in.

"I'm sorry," Norman repeated. "I wanted to make him pay. But I never meant to hurt any of you."

His gaze once again sought out Stephanie. "Frank was my brother, and you were my niece. He talked about you all the time. I couldn't wait to meet you. He said he was bringing you home." The man's voice caught. "Instead I claimed his body."

Tears gleamed in Norman's eyes, and something tugged at Stephanie's heart.

The man looked old and broken, nothing like his picture, nothing like the villain she'd expected.

"I'll get you the rest of the money," Norman told Royce and Jared.

"How?" Royce demanded.

"I gave him a job," said Damien.

"You *what?*" asked Alec.

"I was wrong." Damien shrugged. "He didn't blow the money on women and ponies."

Stephanie moved her attention to her husband.

"No?" Alec asked, watching Damien closely.

Damien gave him a meaningful smile and shook his head. "Let's just say my organization can use his talents."

"Did you steal it from someone else?" Jared demanded.

"It's your money," said Stanton. "I've been holding it for you."

"We'll be looking for interest," Royce put in.

Alec transmitted a silent question to Damien, and Damien's smiled broadened.

Norman's hungry gaze was glued to Stephanie.

She could feel his loneliness and sorrow pierce straight to her soul.

He was her uncle, the brother of a father she didn't remember. She found herself wondering what Royce would do if he thought someone had killed Jared, or the other way around, or what both of them would do if they thought someone had harmed her.

She shifted around Alec, gazing into Norman's lined face in the pool of lamplight.

His eyes went wide, darting to Heidi as she drew closer.

Royce shot forward, but Alec's arm reached out to block him.

Stephanie smiled gently at Norman. "Would you like to meet your grandniece?"

Twin tears slipped out of his blue eyes, trailing swiftly down his pale, sagging cheeks.

Stephanie eased Heidi away from her body, exposing her little pink face. "This is Heidi Rae Creighton. Heidi, this is your uncle Norman."

She felt Alec's gentle hands close around her shoulders.

Norman stood frozen for a full minute.

Then he lifted a shaking finger, gently stroking the back of Heidi's tiny hand. "Heidi Rae." His voice was strangled with emotion.

Stephanie's chest tightened, and tears stung the backs of her eyes.

Royce appeared in Stephanie's peripheral vision. She braced herself, but Royce's body language was no longer hostile.

"This check good?" he asked gruffly.

Norman didn't take his eyes off Heidi. "It's good," he affirmed.

Royce gave a sharp nod as Jared joined them.

Alec's hands squeezed Stephanie's shoulders, and he leaned down to whisper. "You are an amazing woman. And I love you *so* much."

* * * * *

*Harlequin Intrigue top author Delores Fossen
presents a brand-new series of
breathtaking romantic suspense!*
TEXAS MATERNITY: HOSTAGES
*The first installment available May 2010:
THE BABY'S GUARDIAN*

Shaw cursed and hooked his arm around Sabrina.

Despite the urgency that the deadly gunfire created, he tried to be careful with her, and he took the brunt of the fall when he pulled her to the ground. His shoulder hit hard, but he held on tight to his gun so that it wouldn't be jarred from his hand.

Shaw didn't stop there. He crawled over Sabrina, sheltering her pregnant belly with his body, and he came up ready to return fire.

This was obviously a situation he'd wanted to avoid at all cost. He didn't want his baby in the middle of a fight with these armed fugitives, but when they fired that shot, they'd left him no choice. Now, the trick was to get Sabrina safely out of there.

"Get down," someone on the SWAT team yelled from the roof of the adjacent building.

Shaw did. He dropped lower, covering Sabrina as best he could.

There was another shot, but this one came from a rifleman on the SWAT team. Shaw didn't look up, but he heard the sound of glass being blown apart.

The shots continued, all coming from his men, which meant it might be time to try to get Sabrina to better cover. Shaw glanced at the front of the building.

So that Sabrina's pregnant belly wouldn't be smashed

against the ground, Shaw eased off her and moved her to a sitting position so that her back was against the brick wall. They were close. Too close. And face-to-face.

He found himself staring right into those sea-green eyes.

How will Shaw get Sabrina out?
Follow the daring rescue
and the heartbreaking aftermath in
THE BABY'S GUARDIAN
by Delores Fossen,
available May 2010 from Harlequin Intrigue.

is proud to introduce…

New York Times bestselling author

Brenda Jackson

with
SPONTANEOUS

Kim Cannon and Duan Jeffries have a great thing going.
Whenever they meet up, the passion between them
is hot, intense…spontaneous. And things really heat
up when Duan agrees to accompany her to her
mother's wedding. Too bad there's something
he's not telling her….

Don't miss the fireworks!

Available in May 2010
wherever Harlequin Blaze books are sold.

---

red-hot reads

www.eHarlequin.com

HB79542

Bestselling Harlequin Presents® author

Lynne Graham

introduces

VIRGIN ON HER WEDDING NIGHT

Valente Lorenzatto never forgave Caroline Hales's
abandonment of him at the altar. But now he's
made millions and claimed his aristocratic Venetian
birthright—and he's poised to get his revenge.
He'll ruin Caroline's family by buying out their
company and throwing them out of their mansion...
unless she agrees to give him the wedding night
she denied him five years ago....

**Available May 2010
from Harlequin Presents!**

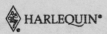
HARLEQUIN®

INTRIGUE

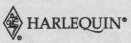

HARLEQUIN®

LAURA MARIE ALTOM

The Baby Twins

Stephanie Olmstead has her hands full raising her twin baby girls on her own. When she runs into old friend Brady Flynn, she's shocked to find herself suddenly attracted to the handsome airline pilot! Will this flyboy be the perfect daddy—or will he crash and burn?

Babies & Bachelors USA

"LOVE, HOME & HAPPINESS"

www.eHarlequin.com

HAR75309

Former bad boy Sloan Hawkins is back in
Redemption, Oklahoma, to help keep his aunt's
cherished garden thriving and to reconnect with the
girl he left behind, Annie Markham. But when he
discovers his secret child—and that single mother
Annie never stopped loving him—he's determined
that a wedding will take place in the garden
nurtured by faith and love.

Where healing flows...

Look for

The Wedding Garden

by Linda Goodnight

Available May 2010
wherever you buy books.

www.SteepleHill.com

REQUEST YOUR FREE BOOKS!

2 FREE NOVELS
PLUS 2
FREE GIFTS!

Silhouette®

Desire®

Passionate, Powerful, Provocative!

YES! Please send me 2 FREE Silhouette Desire® novels and my 2 FREE gifts (gifts are worth about $10). After receiving them, if I don't wish to receive any more books, I can return the shipping statement marked "cancel." If I don't cancel, I will receive 6 brand-new novels every month and be billed just $4.05 per book in the U.S. or $4.74 per book in Canada. That's a saving of at least 15% off the cover price! It's quite a bargain! Shipping and handling is just 50¢ per book.* I understand that accepting the 2 free books and gifts places me under no obligation to buy anything. I can always return a shipment and cancel at any time. Even if I never buy another book, the two free books and gifts are mine to keep forever.

225/326 SDN E5QG

Name _____ (PLEASE PRINT) _____

Address _____ Apt. # _____

City _____ State/Prov. _____ Zip/Postal Code _____

Signature (if under 18, a parent or guardian must sign) _____

Mail to the **Silhouette Reader Service:**

IN U.S.A.: P.O. Box 1867, Buffalo, NY 14240-1867
IN CANADA: P.O. Box 609, Fort Erie, Ontario L2A 5X3

Not valid for current subscribers to Silhouette Desire books.

Want to try two free books from another line?
Call 1-800-873-8635 or visit www.morefreebooks.com.

* Terms and prices subject to change without notice. Prices do not include applicable taxes. N.Y. residents add applicable sales tax. Canadian residents will be charged applicable provincial taxes and GST. Offer not valid in Quebec. This offer is limited to one order per household. All orders subject to approval. Credit or debit balances in a customer's account(s) may be offset by any other outstanding balance owed by or to the customer. Please allow 4 to 6 weeks for delivery. Offer available while quantities last.

Your Privacy: Silhouette Books is committed to protecting your privacy. Our Privacy Policy is available online at www.eHarlequin.com or upon request from the Reader Service. From time to time we make our lists of customers available to reputable third parties who have a product or service of interest to you. If you would prefer we not share your name and address, please check here. ☐

Help us get it right—We strive for accurate, respectful and relevant communications. To clarify or modify your communication preferences, visit us at www.ReaderService.com/consumerschoice.

SDES10R